PUFFIN CANADA

THE POLE

ERIC WALTERS is the highly acclaimed and best-selling author of over fifty novels for children and young adults. His novels have won the Silver Birch Award three times and the Red Maple Award twice, as well as numerous other prizes, including the White Pine, Snow Willow, Tiny Torgi, Ruth Schwartz, and IODE Violet Downey Book Awards, and have received honours from the Canadian Library Association Book Awards, The Children's Book Centre, and UNESCO's international award for Literature in Service of Tolerance.

To find out more about Eric and his novels, or to arrange for him to speak at your school, visit his website at **www.ericwalters.net**.

Also by Eric Walters from Penguin Canada

Victoria,
Go to
90 North!

The Pole
ERIC WALTERS

PUFFIN
CANADA

PUFFIN CANADA

Published by the Penguin Group

Penguin Group (Canada), 90 Eglinton Avenue East, Suite 700, Toronto, Ontario, Canada M4P 2Y3
(a division of Pearson Canada Inc.)

Penguin Group (USA) Inc., 375 Hudson Street, New York, New York 10014, U.S.A.
Penguin Books Ltd, 80 Strand, London WC2R 0RL, England
Penguin Ireland, 25 St Stephen's Green, Dublin 2, Ireland (a division of Penguin Books Ltd)
Penguin Group (Australia), 250 Camberwell Road, Camberwell, Victoria 3124, Australia
(a division of Pearson Australia Group Pty Ltd)
Penguin Books India Pvt Ltd, 11 Community Centre, Panchsheel Park, New Delhi – 110 017, India
Penguin Group (NZ), 67 Apollo Drive, Rosedale, North Shore 0745, Auckland, New Zealand
(a division of Pearson New Zealand Ltd)
Penguin Books (South Africa) (Pty) Ltd, 24 Sturdee Avenue, Rosebank, Johannesburg 2196, South Africa

Penguin Books Ltd, Registered Offices: 80 Strand, London WC2R 0RL, England

Published in Puffin Canada paperback by Penguin Group (Canada),
a division of Pearson Canada Inc., 2008

Published in this edition, 2008

1 2 3 4 5 6 7 8 9 10 (OPM)

Copyright © Eric Walters, 2008

Library and Archives Canada Cataloguing in Publication data available upon
request to the publisher

ISBN: 978-0-14-331248-2

Visit the Penguin Group (Canada) website at **www.penguin.ca**

Special and corporate bulk purchase rates available; please see
www.penguin.ca/corporatesales or call 1-800-810-3104, ext. 477 or 474

The Pole

Chapter One

July 6, 1908

I LEANED against the railing of the ship and took a deep breath. I could faintly make out the salty air of the ocean drifting up the Hudson River. It mingled with, and was nearly overwhelmed by, the thousand other odours that came from the city. There were fumes from the motor cars that raced through the streets, the smells of dozens of different types of cooked or baked foods from countries around the world wafting through the air, and, always, the stink of sewage.

"Ya got time to be lollygaggin'?"

I spun around. It was Captain Bartlett. "No sir, Cap'n, sir. Cookie ordered me out of the galley, sir," I exclaimed. "But I'm sure I can find something else I should 'ave been doing or—"

"It's all right, son, we all know ya been workin' hard," he said, putting a hand on my shoulder. "Takin' a break isn't a bad thing."

"No, sir, it ain't."

"Ain't *ain't* a word, Danny. Use the King's English the way it was intended."

"Yes, sir."

"It's quite a sight, isn't it," Captain Bartlett said, motioning to the skyline of the city that surrounded us.

The whole horizon was filled with buildings. Some of them weren't much, only a few storeys tall, but others soared skyward, more than twenty storeys high.

"Nothing like this back home, not even in St. John's," I said. St. John's was the biggest city in Newfoundland and certainly a whole lot bigger than the outport where I was born and raised—a place that had no more than two hundred people, most of them my relatives in one way or another.

"Nothing like this in the world," Captain Bartlett said. "I heard they have plans to build 'em as high as thirty or even forty storeys."

"That's hard to believe."

"If ya believe it, it can be. Especially here in New York City. Ya know what they call those tall ones?"

I shook my head.

"Skyscrapers, because they go so high that they scrape the sky. And this is just the beginning. Seems like every time I blink my eyes there's a new one goin' up. Look long an' hard at that skyline. By the time we get back it'll be different in a dozen ways."

"How long will it be, sir . . . 'fore we gets back?"

"God willing, we'll push the nose of our ship back into the harbour in fourteen or fifteen months, if the *Roosevelt* can push free of the ice next summer. If she gets wrecked and we have to come south by sledge it's another year more before we return."

I patted the rail of the ship. "She can do it."

"She's a good one," Captain Bartlett agreed. "One hundred and eighty-two feet in length, twelve feet of solid dead wood in the bow, thick keel, close to fifteen hundred horsepower in the engines to push her along, and a hull shaped special to spring over the ice like a steeplechaser taking a fence. Best ship I've ever commanded." He paused. "And despite all of that, the last trip up to the Arctic was practically the death of this girl."

"The *Roosevelt*?" I asked in disbelief.

"Two of the three boilers blew out, we lost our rudder—twice—and the hull was holed. Ran her aground in two places. Should 'ave sunk a dozen times and still managed to limp on back to port in the end."

"But . . . but . . . she looks so strong now."

"Everythin' has been fixed an' made stronger."

"Are we going as far north this time?" I asked hesitantly.

Captain Bartlett nodded. "Cape Sheridan, Arctic Ocean, the farthest north a ship has ever been taken."

"And you took her there the last time," I said.

"There and back," he said proudly. "'Course, gettin' there is just the beginnin'. If all goes well, then Cape Sheridan is just one more step toward the true goal. Now, ya better get yourself ready, here come our guests."

I looked up. Coming down the long pier was a column of cars—big fancy cars. The parade of vehicles slowed down and came to a stop in front of the *Roosevelt*.

Out of the first car stepped Matthew Hensen, our leader's valet and driver. He was a nice man. He was also the first Negro I'd ever met in my life.

He opened up the back door and out stepped Commander Peary, the man leading our expedition. He was wearing the brilliant white uniform of the United States Navy. Free of the car, he placed his hat upon his head.

Standing straight and strong and tall, he looked like a hero. Next came Mrs. Peary, the Commander's wife. Following her was their daughter, Marie, who was nearly fourteen— my age. Finally their son, Robert, came bounding out of the car. His shirt was untucked and his legs were in motion the second they hit the pier. He started running—he was always on the go—before his mother called him back and firmly took his hand. It's hard for a five-year-old to act proper, but I knew that was what was expected of him. He was a good little kid and I talked to him all the time. He was smart as a whip and always asking questions.

Marie stood at her father's side. She was dressed fancy, hat and gloves and all, and she was just about the prettiest girl I ever done seen in my whole—

"Close yer mouth and stop starin'," Captain Bartlett said.

"I wasn't even lookin' at the Commander's daughter!" I protested.

Captain Bartlett chuckled. "If you weren't, how did ya even know I was talkin' about *her*?"

My mind spun trying to come up with an answer. "I've never even talked ta her," I explained.

That was no lie. I didn't have the nerve to dare say a word, or even look her in the eye. 'Course, she was a good three or four inches taller than me, so I'd practically have to be on my tippy-toes to look her square in the eyes. It wasn't that she was really tall or nothing, just that I was sort of on the small side for my age. Who was I kidding? I was a lot on the small side. People sometimes thought I was twelve, or even eleven.

"Keep them eyes to yourself if you don't want the Commander to feed ya to the sharks."

"Yes, sir, Cap'n."

All along the pier people were getting out of their vehicles. There were dozens and dozens, all dressed in fine clothes—fancy dresses and suits and uniforms. They were coming aboard ship to have a small gathering before we set sail.

"Tell Cookie our guests are here."

"Yes, Cap'n, sir."

I rushed across the deck and down the stairs leading to the galley. It was in the middle of the ship, a big room with a table almost as big. I pushed through the swinging door. Cookie was bent over, pulling a tray of biscuits out of the oven.

"Cap'n says to tell ya that our guests are 'ere."

"What does he want ta do about it, come on up on deck and carry 'em along the gangplank?"

I shook my head vigorously. "I just think he wants ya—" I stopped mid-sentence as Cookie broke into a smile and I realized he was only teasing me.

"An' have ya seen hide or hair of the rest of our fine crew?" Cookie asked.

I shook my head. "No, sir."

"Not surprising. Probably arrive as the guests leave. The men wanta get a last little taste a New York 'fore we 'ead north. Can't blame 'em none. If I wasn't here cooking I'd be out on the town meself."

"Me too," I said.

"You? Only way the Cap'n would let ya out is if ya had yourself a babysitter," Cookie said. "Tell the Cap'n I'll be topside soon with the biscuits and pemmican."

"Makes no sense ta me," I said, "why them fancy folks wanta be eating pemmican and biscuits."

"You got something against my biscuits?" he asked angrily, and then he broke into a smile before I could get the wrong idea again.

"I love yer biscuits," I said. "I just mean . . . them people is all rich, so why do they wanta go eating that sort of stuff?"

"They're the ones as put down the money for this ship and those supplies and for the salaries you and me is getting paid. They want a taste of the adventure we's heading out on, an' this is the way they can get a little. Then, in the dark of winter, when they're all snug and safe in their big beds, covered with thick goose-down quilts, lyin' under the warm roofs of their mansions, they can pretend they're in an igloo on the Arctic ice at forty below, listening to the howl of the wind and the barking of the sledge dogs. Does that answer yer question?"

"I guess."

"Good. Now grab a tray of those biscuits and get 'em topside."

"Yes, sir."

The table was covered with trays filled with freshly baked biscuits, some still steaming hot, and slices of pemmican, cold and far from fresh. The pemmican was made of dried meat, fat, and dried berries all pounded together into a gigantic cake. It came in big tins—either bright blue or red—six pounds to a tin.

I reached out and broke off a little piece of pemmican, popping it in my mouth.

"This pemmican ain't fit for hogs!" I exclaimed. "I don't think I can eat this stuff."

"You an' me won't be havin' to eat none of it," Cookie said. "That's the stuff the men'll be eatin' when they sledge north toward the Pole. Me an' you will be safe and warm, sittin' in this 'ere galley with me cookin' and bakin' ta beat the band. Now, off with ya."

I picked up a tray of biscuits and started topside. Balancing the tray with one hand I grabbed a biscuit with the other. It was warm to the touch and I gobbled it down greedily.

Laughter and conversation flooded down the stairway. I stopped at the very top and then peered around the corner. The deck was filled with people, either clustered together talking in groups or strolling about. I suddenly became aware of how shabby my clothes looked and how out of place I'd be up there amongst those fancy folks. Maybe I should just turn tail and go on back and . . . I couldn't do that. Cookie expected me—Cookie had *ordered* me—to bring the food topside. I took a deep breath and stepped out onto the deck. There was hardly any open space and I didn't think I could move to the aft deck to put down the tray without bumping into somebody.

I slipped between people, careful not to touch them or even disturb their conversations. I held the tray firmly. Nothing would be worse than spilling it . . . actually, it would be worse if I spilled it *on* somebody.

"Are these the biscuits we've been promised?"

I looked up at the man standing directly in my path. "Um, yes, sir, these are the biscuits."

"Let us have a taste," he said to the two men standing at his side.

All three took a biscuit.

"Still hot," one of the men said. "Biscuits straight from the oven." He took a bite. "Not bad at all."

The other two agreed.

"Now we have to try some of that pemmican," one of the men said.

"'Fraid ya won't be findin' that so good," I said.

"You've tried it?"

"It's not like the biscuits," I said.

"And where can we find out for ourselves?" the first man asked.

"I'll go and get some. Here," I said, handing him the tray.

He took it, and the other two men laughed.

"Looks like the bank president has become a waiter!" one of them said, and the other roared with laughter.

I suddenly realized what I had done. I tried to take it back.

"That's fine, son. A little honest labour wouldn't hurt any of us. Go and get the pemmican."

I turned and headed back, but I'd gone no more than three steps down the stairs when I practically bumped into Cookie coming up. He was holding a tray of pemmican.

"I'll take it," I said.

He handed me the tray and headed back down to get another. I got back to the deck.

"Danny."

I looked over. It was Mr. Hensen. He motioned for me to come over.

"You don't need to be serving these people," Mr. Hensen said.

"I was just bringin' it up is all, sir, Mr. Hensen, sir, like Cookie told me to do."

"Bring the food up from the aft passage."

"Yes, sir, Mr. Hensen."

"And Danny," he said, "you just call me Matt . . . okay?"

"Yes, sir, Matt."

"I don't see any other members of the crew except Captain Bob."

"Just me and Cookie. Rest are still on shore leave."

He looked at his watch. "Two hours till we weigh anchor. Commander wouldn't want a delay."

"No delay, sir. Cap'n Bartlett told 'em to be 'ere, they'll be 'ere. Nobody would want to get the Cap'n mad at 'em."

"I know *I* wouldn't," Mr. Hensen said, and he laughed. "Captain Bartlett is the best ice captain in the whole world. He's a good man, but one of the toughest I've ever met. You ever see him lose his temper?"

"Just once, and never at me . . . praise the Lord."

"Lucky thing. Now get going and bring the rest of that food up topside."

Chapter Two

COOKIE AND I sat well off to the side and watched as the guests—he called them "the 'igh and mighty"—sampled the biscuits and pemmican.

The biscuits got rave reviews. We could hear what folks were saying, but more telling, we could see their expressions as they came back for seconds and thirds and fourths. There was even one woman who stuffed four or five in her purse. She was a big woman who looked like she'd never missed a meal in her life and sure didn't need any more biscuits.

It was more fun to watch them sampling the pemmican. They'd bite down and their faces would say it all. Some tried to choke it down but others spat it out, either over the rail and into the water or into their hands.

"Look," Cookie whispered. "Here goes another one."

We watched—without trying to be too obvious—as a very dignified woman, dressed all fancy, picked up a piece of pemmican. She put it up to her face and seemed to be smelling it. If she had known that it tasted much worse than it smelled—and it didn't smell very nice at all—she would have just put it back down or tossed it overboard. Instead she put it in her mouth. We could see her chew it and watched in fascination as her eyes bulged and she started to cough and gag. She reached into her purse and pulled out a lacy-looking handkerchief and brought it up to her mouth. Then she delicately folded the handkerchief up and put it back into her purse.

"Guess we knows now how a lady spits out 'er food," Cookie whispered.

"Don't see nobody comin' back for a second piece."

"But those biscuits of mine are doin' good business," Cookie said. "Who knows, maybe after this trip I'll become a cook for the *crème de la crème* of 'igh an' proper society 'ere."

"They could do worse," I agreed.

I liked Cookie. When he gave me orders, most of the time it was more like he was just asking me to do a favour and not yelling at me or nothing. Being the youngest and the smallest—as well as the one with the least experience—aboard ship meant that everybody figured they were my boss. Worse, some people thought they could pass on any job they didn't want to do to me.

Mixed in with the crowd of rich people were a few familiar faces. Along with Commander Peary and his family, Matthew, and Captain Bartlett, there were also the four other members of the expedition. There was Dr. Goodsell, the expedition surgeon, Mr. MacMillan, who was a high school teacher, and Mr. Marvin, who was some sort of university professor. The fourth member, George Borup, hardly seemed that much older than me. He was a student at Cornell University where he was a star athlete. He was big and strong and solid, and he moved like a cat. He was also friendly and always

smiling and givin' me a pat on the back and tellin' jokes.
I liked him a lot.

"Can I have your attention, please!" a loud voice
boomed out. It was Matthew Hensen. "Could we all
assemble on the foredeck?"

I looked over at Cookie to ask if that meant us too, and
he nodded. We got up and trailed behind as the people
shuffled forward.

On the foredeck, standing on a bulkhead—head and
shoulders above the crowd—was Commander Peary. He
raised his hand and the murmur of conversation stopped.

"In two hours, on the next tide, we will weigh anchor
and set forth on an historic mission. On our last trip,
I earned the right to call myself the man who has travelled
the farthest north."

There was a round of applause.

"And while this was a momentous accomplishment, it
was not enough. Our goal for this expedition is simple.
Ninety degrees north, the Pole, nothing else. That is my
pledge."

The audience burst into thunderous applause.
Obviously, this was what they had come to hear.

"But no man could undertake such a mission without
help. I am supported in my quest by the members of our
expedition, by the crew and captain of the *Roosevelt,* and,
perhaps most important, by those of you who are gathered
here today, the members of the Peary Arctic Club.
Without your encouragement, counsel, and generous
support this mission would not be possible."

Commander Peary came to attention, saluted, and then
gracefully bowed from the waist.

"And so, when I stand at the Pole, fulfilling not only my dream, but the dreams of mankind for three centuries, I will not stand alone. You will all be there, standing beside me. To you. My sincere and deepest thanks."

Again, the crowd erupted in applause and cheers of "Hear, hear!" It struck me as sort of funny that they were actually cheering for themselves.

Some of the guests left almost immediately after the Commander had finished his speech. I figured they were hungry and hoping for something better than pemmican to eat. Others lingered longer, but the last few finally departed. And almost like magic, the first members of the crew arrived. I suspected they had been close by, hiding and watching, waiting until the coast was clear. I couldn't really blame them. It was uncomfortable being around all those people. It wasn't that they said or did anything—in fact, they'd basically ignored me—it was just strange to be around people who were so . . . different. Cookie had pointed out some of the jewellery the women were wearing and mentioned how some of those little rings were worth more than the money we'd be earning on this whole trip for a year's worth of work.

As soon as the crew members arrived they started to work, getting the ship ready for departure. Captain Bartlett spoke highly of the crew members. He had hand-picked them, and they were all good Newfoundlanders. Some were from St. John's and others from the little outports and villages that dotted the South Shore. I didn't really know any of them, but if they were from Newfoundland they had to be men who knew the sea.

My attention was caught by motion along the pier. I looked up. There were two motorcycles, ridden by policemen, leading a big, long, black car. Flags—the Stars and Stripes—fluttered from the front fenders of the vehicle. Whoever this was, he had to be important.

The car came to a stop right in front of the *Roosevelt*. The uniformed driver quickly got out and practically raced around to the rear door to open it. He then offered a salute as the passenger emerged. This guy was tall and powerful-looking . . . actually, he looked familiar . . . maybe he had been on the ship before . . . no, that wasn't it.

The two policemen walked behind him as he started up the gangplank of the ship. At that instant I saw that Commander Peary had also noticed our guest. He practically ran across the deck with that awkward gait of his. I'd been told that he lost most of his toes when his feet got frozen on one of his expeditions to the north. I guess it said a lot about his dedication that he was willing to head out again, in spite of that. He stopped at the top end of the gangplank, came to attention, and saluted, just like the driver had done.

"Good afternoon, Commander Peary!" the man called out in a booming voice.

Strange, I thought I even recognized his voice.

"And good afternoon to you, Mr. President!" Commander Peary called back.

That was it—he was the president of the Peary Arctic Club, and he must have been here before. That would explain why he was so important . . . but important enough to have policemen on motorcycles escort him around?

The man—the president—walked up the gangplank, closely followed by two other men who had emerged from the car, with both police officers in hot pursuit.

"Permission to board, Commander Peary?" he asked.

"Permission granted. It is our honour to have you aboard."

At this point he walked onto the deck and the two men shook hands. I stood there, off to the side, watching as they began talking—too quietly for me to hear—and wondered if I should finish cleaning up or if I should leave out the remaining biscuits and pemmican and lemonade in case he wanted to sample them.

"Boy!" Commander Peary called, and I started out of my thoughts.

"Bring coffee, a whole pot, and some cups, to my cabin. You can show these gentlemen to the galley," he said, indicating the two men who had been in the car, "and ask Cookie to make sure they are taken care of."

"Yes, sir."

I grabbed one of the remaining trays and hurried down to the galley, leading the way for the two men. When I got there, Cookie was bent over the sink, scrubbing away at the baking pans.

"Got to get some coffee for the Commander and his guests," I announced. "And the Commander asks would you fix something for these gentlemen as well." The two men sat down, silent as ever.

"More guests? I thought they'd all left," Cookie said.

"Just one car's worth. They want coffee."

He motioned to the stove. There was a pot percolating on the top.

"Use a tray, an' take lots of cups."

"I only need a few cups."

"What if Mrs. Peary wants a cup? Ya gonna make 'er drink from the pot?" Cookie asked.

I took the tray I'd been carrying, emptying it of the last few biscuits. I popped one of them in my mouth. Then I grabbed seven mugs out of the cupboard and put them on the tray, along with the coffee pot, some spoons, a little jug of cream, and a sugar bowl.

"Get in an' get out an' don't be sayin' too much," Cookie warned me.

"I won't be sayin' nothin' but *'Ere's the coffee*."

The Commander's cabin was close to the galley. There at the door, one on either side, backs against the wall, were the two police officers. They stood, still as statues, staring straight ahead. I could hear ragtime music playing through the door.

"Coffee," I said, explaining why I was there. One of them nodded.

I knocked.

"Come!"

I opened the door and entered. Commander Peary, the president man, and Captain Bartlett were sitting at a small table in the corner of the cabin. It was a beautiful cabin, all yellow pine, with a big pianola—which was playing the music—and a large bed. I knew he even had his own private head with a bathtub.

"Put it down right here, Danny," Captain Bartlett said, motioning to the side table.

Carefully I put the tray down. "Do you want me to pour?" I asked.

"Nice of ya to offer," Captain Bartlett said. "All black, right?"

Both men agreed, and while I started to pour they picked up their conversation.

"So, tell me the details of your assault on the Pole."

"We hope to make Cape Sheridan by the first week in September," Commander Peary replied.

"Is that where you landed on your last attempt?"

"One an' the same," Captain Bartlett said.

"The farthest north a ship has ever been taken and returned," Commander Peary pointed out. "A testament to the man who captained her. Without Captain Bartlett, I would never have achieved the title of farthest man north."

"An accomplishment of great merit," the president guy said. "But of course this time you are not seeking merely to be *farther* north but the *farthest possible* north. The attainment of the Pole should be your main object. Nothing short of that will suffice."

"On this, we agree," Commander Peary said.

"It's ninety or nothin'," Captain Bartlett added. "The North Pole or bust."

Trying not to interrupt, I put down two mugs of steaming coffee—one for the president and the other for Commander Peary.

I went back to get the third mug for Captain Bartlett, and as I walked my eye was caught by the large portrait on the wall behind them. I stopped dead in my tracks. I looked at the painting, and then at the man, and then back at the painting. It was *him,* the man . . . and on the frame was a little plaque saying who he was. This man wasn't the president of the Peary Arctic Club . . . he was the President of *the United States of America*! This was President Roosevelt!

The mug almost slipped through my fingers.

"Ya bringin' me that coffee?"

"Yes, sir." Suddenly I was very aware of my feet and not wanting to trip over them.

"So, Danny," the man—the *President*—said, "you must be the youngest member of this expedition."

"Yes, sir."

"How old are you?"

"Fourteen, sir."

"Isn't that the same age as your oldest, your daughter?" he asked the Commander.

"She'll be fourteen in September, Mr. President."

"I don't suppose you'd allow her to travel with you on one of these expeditions," he said.

Commander Peary scoffed. "It isn't a fitting place for a woman, young or old. Besides, she would miss far too much school."

He turned back to me. "How about your school, Danny?"

I shook my head. "My schooling's all done."

"But hopefully not all your education. Most of what is important I learned not from school but from life. Wouldn't you agree, gentlemen?"

They both did, although I had the feeling that they would have agreed with pretty much anything he said.

"You are a very fortunate young man to be part of such an adventure at such a tender age," he said.

"Yes, sir."

He pulled a big gold watch from his vest pocket and opened it up. "It is time for me to take my leave. Gentlemen, Godspeed."

Chapter Three

July 8, 1908

THE BOAT was bucking and rocking, bounced by the waves and strong headwinds. The deck was slippery from the spray and I kept one hand on the railing as I moved along the deck. I could feel the spray against my face, while the rest of my body was protected by the heavy slicker that I wore over my clothing. The moon and stars were hidden by clouds and the only light was coming from the portholes of the topside cabins.

Carefully, slowly, I moved toward the foredeck. I guess I should have stayed inside but I was feeling a little bit queasy—it had been two days but I still hadn't gotten my sea legs, or, more important, my sea stomach . . . a fact that some of the other sailors had noticed. Some of the men treated me well. Others called me things like "half-pint" or "squirt" and seemed to like to make fun of me. There were a couple that I would have enjoyed throwing up on, but being outside was easier on my stomach, and if I did get sick again nobody would be the wiser.

I gripped the railing tight and used it not only to steady me, but to pull myself forward as I worked my way slowly toward the foredeck.

"What are ya doin' up 'ere?" a voice called out. It was one of the sailors—Keith—standing against the rail in his black slicker. I hadn't even noticed him, even though I was practically on top of him.

"Just gettin' some air," I explained.

"Lots of air down below, an' that's where you should be."

"I'll go down soon."

"I'd be down there right now if I wasn't on watch. You be careful, it's not safe to be up 'ere in conditions like these. Don't want to be tryin' to fish ya out of the drink . . . that's assumin' somebody would even see ya goin' overboard in the first place."

I looked over the side. I could just make out the tops of the waves as the cold, dark water rushed by. I felt a shudder go up my spine that had nothing to with the wind or the spray.

"I'll be all right."

He patted me on the back as I moved by. There were always at least three men on duty all the time: one on the bridge steering, a second navigating, and a third man on watch.

With even greater care I kept moving forward. I worked my way around the cabin and finally slumped down on the foredeck. There was a slight overhang so I was a little bit sheltered from the spray and safely away from the rail. I wouldn't stay out long—just long enough to get some fresh air and try to settle my stomach.

We'd been at sea for two days. It would be another two or three days before we reached Sydney, Nova

Scotia. There we'd be putting in for coal and to let off Mrs. Peary and the children. They'd be travelling back down to New York by train. I could understand them wanting to be onboard for the first leg of the trip, though. Even if things went perfectly, Commander Peary would be gone from his family for at least a year. It would be hard not to see your father for that long . . . or to never see him again . . . I couldn't let my mind go flying off in that direction—there was no point in dwelling on what couldn't be . . .

I thought I heard somebody scream! The wind could sure play some funny tricks when it was whipping around the lines and the rigging and—there it was again! I couldn't see anything from my little protected perch. I braced myself against the cabin and unsteadily got to my feet again. Where had that voice come from? Was it really a voice or—I heard it again . . . somewhere off to the port side. I moved around the corner and took a few steps and there, lying on the deck, was a body! I stumbled forward, practically tripping over top of it.

"Are you okay?" I yelled as I dropped to my knees. I kept one hand on the lower railing and reached out to help with the other.

The slicker-covered figure raised its head—it was Marie Peary! Even in the dim light I could see a look of total terror on her face.

I rose to my feet, pulling her up, and then the ship bucked and the two of us were tossed forward and to the side. My body absorbed the blow as we crashed into the cabin and bounced down, hitting the deck again, this time with me collapsing right on top of her. She let out a scream and then a groan as I landed on her. We were a tangle of arms and legs, and as hard as I tried to separate us she was clinging to me for all she was worth.

"We 'ave to get inside!" I screamed into her ear.

"I'm scared!"

"Nothin' to be ascared of!" I yelled. "Just take my hand."

She grabbed my hand and I rolled off to the side. For a split second my leg slipped under the lower railing and I felt myself panic. I pulled it back in and grabbed on, using the railing to pull myself up. I dragged her to her feet and we stumbled and staggered a few steps before her legs went out from under her and she fell headfirst into the cabin wall! She slumped down to her knees, and only my grip stopped her from going down completely.

"Stay down!" I yelled. "Stay on your knees . . . crawl!"

I hovered over top of her, a hand on one cabin wall, bracing myself against the other, waiting for the next jolt. The deck was slick and I had trouble keeping my feet under me as I struggled to move her along. She was dead weight. Practically dragging her behind me, I grabbed the cabin door and with a burst of strength pushed her inside, then tumbled over on top of her. We were inside and safe!

She started crying, big, deep sobs.

"Are ya hurt?"

She shook her head but kept on sobbing. I slammed the hatch door closed, sealing us in and the storm out.

"We're safe . . . ya don't have to cry no more."

She nodded in agreement. The tears were starting to slow down.

"Just sit 'ere," I said. "I'm goin' to get yer father."

I SAT IN THE GALLEY, a blanket wrapped tightly around my shoulders. I had changed out of my wet clothing but I was still feeling all shaky and shivery—I didn't think it had to do with being cold any more. Cookie was over by the stove and Captain Bartlett paced back and forth the length of the room. Having Cookie there made me comfortable. Having the Captain there was making me nervous. He hadn't said a word to me, and the longer he went without speaking the worse I figured it would be when he started. I'd heard the Captain lose his temper before. The words flew fast and furious and were so blistering that they could peel the paint from a wall or the barnacles from the keel of a ship.

"This will take away the shakes," Cookie said as he handed me a steaming mug.

"Maybe that isn't such a good idea," Captain Bartlett said, finally finding words.

We both gave him a questioning look.

"I think the shakes might be good for the lad . . . might shake some sense into him, because he can't have much goin' on up in that head of his!"

I knew it was coming now. I braced myself.

"Can you tell me, boy, what in the name of the good Lord were ya doin' on deck in a storm like that?" he demanded.

"I don't know, sir. I know I shouldn't 'ave been up there, sir," I apologized.

"So you had no good reason, is that what you're sayin'?" he asked angrily.

I shook my head.

He started yelling and screaming, throwing in words that I knew had never been heard inside of no church. I kept my head down and just said "Yes, sir" or "No, sir" when I thought he wanted me to answer.

"An' bad enough puttin' yourself at risk, why did ya have to put Marie at risk too? You should know better . . . couldn't ya have thought up a better place to meet with her?"

"What?" I asked, understanding the words but not what he meant.

"Meeting her. Couldn't the two of ya met down below?" he demanded angrily.

"But we weren't meetin' anywhere . . . we was both just up there," I stammered.

"Do ya think that I'm the one that's the idiot?" he screamed. "Ya don't think I can remember what it was like to be a lad and wantin' to see a young lassie who ya like and—"

"But it wasn't like that!" I protested. "I wasn't meetin' with 'er, it was just that we was both up on the deck is all!"

"Bad enough ya risked the lives of two people, but don't ya go lyin' ta me now, boy!"

"But I'm not lying!" I protested. "Honest!"

The Captain opened his mouth to say something and then stopped. He came closer until he was standing right over top of me and looking down. It was an angry stare, but at least he wasn't yelling—for a few seconds. I tried to keep looking him straight in the eye—I knew that liars looked away—but his stare was too fierce and I finally lowered my eyes to the floor.

"Do ya mean to tell me that it was just chance that the two of ya were up there on the deck?" he asked. His words were suddenly quiet and measured—somehow that seemed even more frightening.

"Yes, sir, chance, sir."

"Do you swear ta God that that is the truth?"

"Ta God, on a stack of Bibles, sir, it's God's own truth."

He straightened up and started to stroke his face with his hand. He looked like he was thinking. He slowly walked away and I felt like a pressure—the pressure of his presence—was lifted off my chest. He stopped at the stove and poured himself a coffee. He walked back over, pulled out a chair, and sat down on the far side of the table.

"Right now the Commander is talkin' with his daughter. Do ya think she's goin' to tell the same story as you?"

"She'll say the same thing 'cause it ain't no story, it's the truth."

He took a long sip from his coffee but didn't say anything.

"You 'ave to believe me, sir!" I protested.

"I'm the Cap'n of this ship so I don't have to do anythin' . . . but I *do* believe you."

A wave of relief washed over my body.

"What do ya think would have happened to young Marie if ya hadn't come upon her?" he asked.

"I don't know, sir," I said, shaking my head. "She might 'ave gotten back inside by 'erself."

"Or might not." He took a big sip from his mug. "Ya shouldn't have been up on the deck," he said slowly, "and if ya ever go topside durin' a storm like that again, I'll personally *throw* ya over the side."

"Yes, sir, ya 'ave my word that I won't . . . " I heard the sound of the galley hatch opening and I turned around. It was Commander Peary. I struggled to get to my feet but before I could rise I felt his hand on my shoulder.

"Sit . . . please," he said, and nervously I settled back down into the seat.

He pulled out a chair and sat down beside me.

"Cookie," he said, "may I have a cup of your steaming java?"

"Sure can, sir."

Cookie poured the Commander a mug and placed it beside him.

"How are you feeling, son?"

"I'm fine. How is Marie?"

"She's a little distraught, but fine . . . thanks to you."

"I didn't do anythin'," I said.

"If not for you my daughter could have been lost."

"I just helped get 'er inside . . . done what anybody would have done."

"But it wasn't anybody, it was you. I am in your debt. And, as God is my witness, I will honour that debt, although there is nothing that could ever repay such a deed."

He reached out and took my hand in his. "At some time, perhaps it will be years from now, if you require my assistance in any matter, no matter how small and insignificant or impossibly large, you may contact me, and whatever is within my reach or resources will be done. You have my word."

"Thank you, sir."

He released my hand. "Now, it is time to retire for the evening." He got up. "Good night, and again, my thanks, and my word—at some time in the future, you may be in need of my assistance."

I quickly got to my feet. "Good night, sir."

He departed, leaving me and Cookie and the Captain alone in the room. I closed my eyes and thought about what Commander Peary had just said. It was all going to be all right.

"More coffee?" Cookie asked the Captain.

The Captain held up his cup. Cookie walked over and refilled first the Captain's mug and then mine.

"It's a shame," Captain Bartlett said.

"What is?" Cookie asked.

"It's a shame for the boy here," he said, motioning to me, "that it's *me* who's in charge of him instead of Commander Peary. Commander wants to give him a medal . . . Me? I'm not sure if he should be toasted or have his bottom tanned."

My feeling of relief was now gone.

"How is the boy doin' down here?" Captain Bartlett asked Cookie. "Is he doing his job?"

"I've 'ad worse and I've 'ad better."

Those weren't the words I'd been hoping for to defend me.

"Could ya get by without him?"

"Might be easier without 'im under me feet some of the time," Cookie said.

This was starting to look worse and worse . . . was he going to be punishing me? Was he going to fire me?

"When we arrive in Sydney, ya will no longer be employed by this ship as a cook's assistant an' cabin boy."

I couldn't believe my ears. He was firing me! I felt like I was going to cry. How would I get back to Newfoundland, and what would I say to my sister, and—

"You'll no longer be a cabin boy, because I'm givin' ya a promotion. Seaman . . . third class."

Chapter Four

I LOOKED UP. Every inch of canvas that could be hung from the three masts was bulging in the breeze and we were moving at a tremendous clip—that was good . . . but dangerous.

Three days ago we had seen our first iceberg. It wasn't much more than just a distant shape on the horizon—tiny, hardly noticeable—and then it vanished as quickly as it had appeared. As it continued to drift south, we sailed north. The second one was different. It was a mountain of ice that appeared just off the port side. I stood there on the deck, looking up, up, up at the berg, which towered well above the tallest tip of our middle mast. If it hadn't been so deadly I would have said it was beautiful, a dozen different shades of white and blue, and the way the light played off it was a sight to behold. We tacked well to the side but it was so massive that standing there on the deck I could feel the change in the air as it cooled down dramatically.

Since that first sighting the watch had been tripled— two men on the deck and a third up at the top of the tallest mast in the crow's nest. It seemed like most of the time the man up top was Captain Bartlett himself—sometimes for ten or twelve hours at a stretch. He was up there now. I looked up through the sails. I could just see the outline of the Captain's head above the barrel.

"Hey, Danny!" It was Angus, one of the crew. "Are you still the cook's assistant or are you a sailor?"

"I'm a little of both," I answered.

"Hopin' you'd be sayin' that. Here," he said, offering me a small canvas sack he was carrying.

"What is it?" I asked as I took it.

"Supper."

"But I've already eaten."

"Not for you . . . for 'im," he said, pointing upward.

For a few seconds I thought he meant God, but then I realized he meant the Captain.

"Cap'n Bob 'asn't eaten yet. Bring it up to 'im."

"Me?"

"Unless you're ascared of heights," he said.

"I'm not ascared of nothin'!" I protested.

"Good. Sling the bag over your shoulder an' climb up the riggin'."

"No problem. Nothin' to it." Without another word I turned and walked away, leaving Angus—and any worries I might show—behind me. I didn't want to give anybody any excuse to say anything about me not doing my job.

Ever since I'd been promoted to sailor, some members of the crew had given me an even harder time. Not all. Most were pretty good, but some had lots of comments—about my age and my size and how I didn't deserve to be promoted. Funny how the emptiest heads can make the most noise.

I walked along the deck and over to the rigging that led from the railing up to the crow's nest. I looked up. Way up. I'd seen crew members moving along the rigging—some scrambled like monkeys—to work the sails. I'd seen it. I'd just never done it. How hard could it be, though? I'd climbed enough trees in my time. Then again, none of those trees were moving. I was suddenly even more grateful for the calm seas.

I reached up and grabbed the rigging, testing it with my hand—strong, and securely fastened. I looked over the side. The water was rushing by. I grabbed the rigging and swung myself up.

I took a deep breath and then started to climb. Slowly, carefully, deliberately. I made sure that I always had one hand firmly gripping the ropes before I moved the other hand. Always had one foot firmly anchored on one step before I moved my other foot up to the next. Hand over hand I inched upward.

The wind was getting stronger and the sound of the sails flapping in the breeze became louder in my ears. The boat pitched and I felt a rush of fear race through my body. I gripped the rigging as if my life depended on it . . . after all, my life *did* depend on it.

I looked down through the ropes, frozen in place. Were the seas suddenly getting rougher, or was it just that I was climbing higher and that made it feel like the swells were getting bigger?

Far below was the deck. If I lost my grip and fell I'd be killed instantly. I'd break my neck. But if I started to fall and then pushed off, maybe I could clear the deck and hit the water instead. I could survive if I hit the water. Of course, if nobody saw me fall into the water I'd drown . . . no, I'd probably freeze to death first. I drove that thought out of my head. I wasn't going to fall. But I couldn't stay where I was forever. Up or down? No, there was no choice. I wasn't going down. If I went back down now I was finished as a seaman and I might as well go back down to the galley and learn to cook.

I took a deep breath. I had to think about what I had to do, think about climbing up. I unhooked my left hand and reached up to the next rung. I pulled myself up. I gripped the rope tightly and moved my right hand up, stepping up to the next rung. Rung by rung, hand over hand, I was climbing. I looked up. I was practically there.

"Who is that?" Captain Bartlett's voice came down from above.

"It's me, Cap'n . . . Danny."

"Danny, what are ya doin' comin' up here?"

"Bringin' your supper, sir."

"Good. I'm hungry as a bear."

I climbed up the final few rungs until my head was level with the top of the barrel of the crow's nest. Captain Bartlett reached out and offered me his hand. I took it and I was yanked up and pulled right into the barrel! Still holding me in a vise-like grip he plopped me down and my feet hit the bottom.

"Thought I'd give ya a little helpin' hand," he said. "Now, how about givin' me my supper?"

"Sure, of course, sir." I pulled the bag off my shoulder and handed it to the Captain.

He reached inside and pulled out a big sandwich. "Was hopin' for somethin' hot, but I knew that wasn't goin' to be happenin' as I saw ya start to climb."

I gave him a questioning look.

"Speed ya was travellin' it was goin' be cold by the time I got it no matter how hot it was when it left the galley." He chuckled. "One point there I thought I'd have ta come on down an' shake ya awake."

"I was just bein' careful."

"Careful is good." He took a big bite from his sandwich and then reached into the bag and removed a clear glass bottle. It looked like coffee. He unscrewed the lid and brought it up to his face and inhaled.

"Ahhhh . . . as long as the coffee is hot, nothin' else matters." He took a sip.

The Captain drank pots and pots of coffee every day. I'd never even seen him drink anything else—not tea, not beer, not even a shot of rum. It was pretty unusual for a sailor—and even stranger for a sailor from Newfoundland. My mother used to say that for a ship from Newfoundland to run there had to be wind in its sails and screech or rum in the bellies of the crew.

"Ever been up here before?" he asked.

"Never been in the rigging before."

"Guess I should 'ave figured that out. Nice up here. Peaceful. Wonderful view. Look," he said, pointing off to the port side. "Do you see it?"

I started back to attention. Was there an iceberg up ahead? I shaded my eyes and stared into the distance, scanning the seas. I didn't see any icebergs. I didn't see anything . . . no, there was a thin, dark line that stretched across the horizon.

"Greenland," he said. "She moved into view about three hours ago. Do ya know why it's called Greenland?"

"No," I said, shaking my head.

"Place was discovered by a Viking. Leif Ericsson. He wanted people to come and settle so he figured he had to make it sound nice. He called it Greenland even though there's not much more than ice and snow, gravel and rock." He took a drink from his coffee. "Still, beautiful place in its own way. Coast is lined with fjords and glaciers. These bergs we've been dodging are mainly calved in those fjords."

"I didn't know that."

"Ya know, on a day like this, when it isn't too cold and it's dry, there isn't a much better place ta be in the whole world."

"You're spending a lot of time here."

"No choice. Don't think I've ever seen so many bergs in my life."

"I've only seen a few," I said.

"That's because I've seen 'em first an' had us change course. But by midday we'll have a break from the bergs. We'll be puttin' inta the Etah Fjord."

"Why are we stoppin' there?"

"That's where we'll be gettin' the rest of the members of our expedition, the people who are goin' ta be doin' most of the work . . . the Eskimos." He took a sip from his coffee. "You ever seen an Eskimo?"

"Never."

"You're gonna be seein' a lot of 'em over the next ten months. I think you'll like 'em. 'Course, everybody is different, their own person, but as a whole you won't find a nicer, gentler group of people in the world. Treat each other with respect, love their children, share with each other." He chuckled. "Funny, not a Christian amongst 'em but they sure do understand what bein' a good Christian is about. Ya go to church back home?" he asked.

I suddenly felt uncomfortable. "We used to . . . before."

"Before what?"

"Before my father died."

"An' then?"

"An' then me Mom said she didn't believe in God no more so she wouldn't be goin' ta church again."

"And you?"

"I didn't go to church either."

"But do you believe in God?"

"I . . . I . . . I guess I do."

The Captain didn't say anything and the silence felt heavy and tense.

"Did ya know that I almost became a Methodist minister?"

"You?"

"Don't sound so surprised."

"I'm not surprised . . . well not *that* surprised." I was trying to picture this man who could scream out a lungful of profanities as a minister. Certainly if he'd used any of those words up in the pulpit it would have made for a pretty interesting sermon. I would have gone to church to hear that.

"Two years I studied," he said. "It was what my mother wanted." He shook his head. "Wasn't right for me. I was meant to be out 'ere . . . on the ocean . . . on the ice." He paused again. "I've spent a fair amount of time in churches. Funny, sometimes I felt God's presence in church, and sometimes I didn't. But up north I can always feel Him. I can almost hear Him whisper in my ears. If ya listen closely, maybe you'll hear Him whisper too."

I didn't know what to say. I just felt uncomfortable. I needed to change the subject.

"Do the Eskimos speak English?" I asked.

"Most speak a few words. Some speak more. A couple speak English pretty good. Maybe you'll learn some of their language. It's called Inuktitut."

"Can you speak it?"

"Enough to get across what I need to get across. Hopefully you'll be learnin' some yourself. Speakin' of learnin', I hear you're learnin' pretty fast."

"Who said that?" I asked.

"Angus, Keith, my first mate, just about everybody aboard ship. They all have good things ta say."

That made me feel good. Even if they were saying some things *to* me that weren't nice, at least the things they were saying *about* me were good. There were lots of things to learn, and I was trying my best.

I looked out at the view Captain Bartlett enjoyed so much. It was beautiful. Blue, blue sky, dark, greenish water and . . . what was that? Small, and on the cusp of the horizon.

"I see something . . . out there."

"Where?"

I pointed out in front, just off the starboard side.

"I don't see anything," Captain Bartlett said.

"It's there, just small, but on the horizon."

"Light and water can play tricks on the eyes."

I shook my head. "No, there's something there, look."

The Captain had a pair of binoculars around his neck. He brought them up to his eyes. He swept the binoculars around, trying to locate what I saw . . . or, at least, what I *thought* I saw.

He lowered the binoculars and then pulled them off his neck. "Here," he said, offering them to me.

I took them and looked at the spot where I still thought I could see something. It felt strange looking through them, and I couldn't make out anything but a blur of water.

"I . . . I . . . can't see anything."

He took the binoculars back. "You don't need 'em. You saw it with your naked eye."

"I saw something . . . I can *still* see something out there. Is it a berg?"

"Big one. Still three or four miles away. Close as we're gonna get." He leaned over the side of the crow's nest. "Ten degrees to port!" he yelled.

"Ten degrees port!" I heard another voice call out, relaying his order to the bridge.

"Now, I have one more thing for ya to do," Captain Bartlett said. "Ya can go and tell the Commander that we will be droppin' anchor in Etah by midday tomorrow."

"Yes, sir." I took hold of the rigging and pulled myself up and onto it and out of the crow's nest.

"An' boy . . . thanks for bringin' up my supper . . . an' for the conversation."

Chapter Five

I KNEW EXACTLY WHERE to find Commander Peary. It was just after six bells. He and the other members of his expedition would be in the galley, eating dinner. The rest of the crew ate in shifts—some earlier in the day and others much later—but the Commander always ate at the same time.

I paused just before I reached the hatch to the galley. Commander Peary had always been polite to me, and since that night I'd saved his daughter he had been *very* nice to me, but he still made me a little nervous. He was a famous Arctic explorer and the commander of our expedition and I was just a cabin boy . . . no, I reminded myself, a Seaman, third class. I opened up the hatch.

"Danny!" Commander Peary yelled out a greeting and the other men nodded or smiled or waved. Doc Goodsell and Mr. Marvin sat beside the Commander and Mr. MacMillan, and George, the university student, sat across the table. Matt stood off to one side. Cookie wasn't there. It was strange for him not to be there.

"Hello, sir. May I come in?"

"Of course you may. Please come and join us!"

"Thank you, sir. I have a message from Cap'n Bartlett. He said for me to tell ya that we'll be makin' Etah by the afternoon of tomorrow."

"Excellent news!" the Commander said. "That puts us at least two days ahead of schedule. Now, for more immediate matters. Have you eaten, Danny?"

"Yes, sir. I ate with the crew around four bells."

"Four bells is a long time ago, surely you'd like something more."

"Well . . . I guess . . . " I took a step toward the stove and—

"Matthew, get Danny some grub."

I stopped. "I can get it," I offered.

"No, you come, have a seat," he said, gesturing to an empty chair at the end of the table. "Matthew will serve you . . . that's why he's here."

I sat down, but I felt really uncomfortable.

Matt walked over to the cupboard and took out a bowl. Then he removed the lid from a big pot of stew that was simmering on the stove. He ladled out a heaping helping and brought it over, placing it in front of me.

"Thanks," I said.

Matt nodded.

"I could use more, myself," Mr. Marvin said as he held up his bowl to Matt.

"It will be an eventful day tomorrow," Commander Peary said.

"More than just eventful," George exclaimed. "It will be thrilling!" That was just like George, to be so excited. He was more like a little kid than a man in some ways, always happy and smiling and friendly.

"This will be my first opportunity to meet a Native, a noble Eskimo," George said.

"They are an interesting people," Commander Peary told him. "Uneducated, but wise in the ways of the Arctic and survival. Completely lacking in what we would define as civilization, but possessing their own unique culture. Gentle but savage. Heathens with no true understanding of *real* religion but in many ways following the lessons of Christ."

"That's what the Cap'n said . . . about the religion part."

"Captain Bartlett would know. He is one of the few people onboard who has had any contact with the Eskimos. The others being myself, of course, and Matt."

"Nobody else?" I asked, looking around the table.

The four men sitting at the table shook their heads. They almost looked embarrassed.

"In fact, this is the farthest north any of these men has ever travelled before," Commander Peary said.

I was shocked, and my expression must have given me away.

"You looked surprised," Commander Peary said.

"Not surprised, sir. It was just . . . just . . . not what I 'ad expected."

"Have no concerns," Commander Peary said. "These are strong, resourceful, determined men, and as long as they take my directions we shall succeed. And, of course, we are being captained by the man who was in command of the *Roosevelt* on her last mission north. Captain Bartlett is perhaps the greatest ice captain alive."

He didn't have to convince me about the Captain. All of the crew had complete confidence in him.

"And don't forget Matt, here," George said. "How many times have you been to the Arctic, Matt?"

"I've accompanied the Commander on each of his Arctic trips," Matt answered quietly.

"I guess that would make you one of the most experienced Arctic travellers in history," George said.

"One of," he agreed.

"Matthew certainly knows the Arctic," Commander Peary agreed. "Hardly a man alive who knows more about the Arctic than my faithful valet. I'd trust my life in the hands of this man." He paused. "Actually I *have* put my life in his hands, on more occasions than I can count."

"As I have put my life in your hands," Matt said. As he spoke, he came over with the bowl of stew for Mr. Marvin. He set it down, and Mr. Marvin nodded his approval.

This all seemed strange. Here was the person who had the most Arctic experience—as much as Commander Peary—and he was serving everybody instead of sitting down and eating with everybody else.

"I have an idea," George said. "How about if we have young Danny here accompany us when we put in at Etah? He could come ashore and meet the Eskimos!"

Commander Peary turned to me. "Would you like that?"

"I don't know . . . the Cap'n might need me aboard ship . . . "

"I'll speak to him. I'm sure he can spare you. It would be a wonderful opportunity to explore a Native community . . . highly educational. Now, first things, first. Do you have anything warmer than the coat you're wearing now?"

"No, sir."

"We must remedy that. Matthew, take Danny down to the supplies as soon as possible and get him some furs."

August 16, 1908

I leaned against the railing, looking out on the isolated community. Etah certainly was a great deal different from our last ports. It made Sydney, Nova Scotia, look like New York City. There was a series of haphazardly placed structures—nothing more than stones piled on top of stones, one storey tall. Each one looked about large enough to house a few people in one room. The buildings looked particularly small against the rocky cliffs that rose up behind them. I could make out some movement—tiny people moving between the buildings—and there were three or four plumes of smoke rising up in scattered locations across the settlement.

There was also a sound, carried by the stiff winds blowing from the land. At first it was so faint that I didn't even recognize it. Then, as I pulled down my hood, perked my ears, and focused my thoughts, I realized what it was. It was the sound of dogs barking . . . sledge dogs.

I pulled my hood back up. It was hard to believe it could be this chilly in the middle of August. Especially since the sun was shining so brightly—and for almost twenty-four hours a day!

"You ready, Danny?" Commander Peary asked as he came up beside me.

"Yes, sir."

"Let's make for the dory."

I followed the Commander. A large dory had been lowered into the water and we climbed down a set of stairs to get to it. In the boat already were the Doc, George, Mr. MacMillan—who had asked me to call him Donald—and Mr. Marvin, who I wouldn't have dreamed of calling anything but "Sir" or "Mister." Matt was standing at the stern, manning the tiller, and four crewmen— including Keith and Angus—were at the oars ready to row. I was surprised that the Captain wasn't with us, but I understood he had plenty of things to do aboard ship. I took a seat right up in the bow.

Lines were cast off and we started rowing. I watched intently as the shore became larger and larger and I could make out more detail. As we got closer, more people began to appear, spilling out of the shelters. They were coming out to see us land. I tried to do a rough count but their growing ranks made that impossible. There had to be at least two hundred or more people standing on the stony beach!

As we neared the shore, Peary stood up in the boat. He wobbled, and for a split second I thought he was going to tumble over before Matt reached out and offered a hand, steadying him.

"Good afternoon, my fine friends!" the Commander yelled out.

They waved back, and called out things I couldn't understand. What I could see was that they seemed really happy to see him—lots of waves and big, bright smiles.

The boat ran aground on the rocky shallows, and again the Commander almost toppled forward, steadied by both Matt and George this time. Two of the crew jumped out and pulled the dory up and onto the stony shore, beaching it.

As soon as Commander Peary had climbed out he was mobbed by Natives, who surged forward and offered outstretched hands and greetings. One by one our party piled out of the boat and onto the shore. The crew then hauled the empty dory right up and out of the water, the bottom calling out in noisy protest as the wooden keel scraped against the rocks.

The Commander stood beside one man—one Eskimo. He looked really old, but I thought that he must be important. Maybe he was like the mayor or leader or whatever Eskimos have. One by one Peary introduced him to the four members of his expedition. I stood by the dory with the rest of the crew. Off to the side stood Matt, and while there were no other members of our party with him he was surrounded by people, by Eskimos. While Commander Peary was shaking hands, slapping a back here and there, Matt was being offered hugs and kisses and was practically being mobbed. Peary's welcome was warm, but Matt was being embraced like a long-lost family member.

Peary started to walk away and everybody trailed after him—the Eskimos and the members of the expedition. Matt broke free and started after Peary as well. I thought I'd just stay at the dory with the crew.

"Danny!" Peary yelled, startling me. "Come!" And I ran after him.

I fell into line behind Matt. I noticed then for the first time that Matt was carrying a bag over his shoulder. It looked heavy, and it made a clanking sound as he moved.

"What's in the bag?" I asked.

"My lunch."

"But didn't you eat on the . . . ?" I let the sentence trail off as Matt broke into a big smile and I realized he was just kidding me.

"Stay close and you'll see," Matt said. He didn't need to say that again. I was planning on staying very close.

Everybody said how nice the Eskimos were—and they sure seemed friendly—but I felt nervous. Everything was so different, and I didn't understand a word anybody was saying, and to make it all worse my legs felt strange . . . it was hard getting my land legs back after being aboard ship for so long. It felt like the ground was moving, swaying underneath me.

The people weren't tall—a lot were barely taller than me—and they were all dressed strangely in skins. I noticed they had olive skin, hair as dark as night, and teeth as white as snow. The teeth stood out because everybody seemed to be smiling.

There were also lots of dogs, tied to stakes in the ground, beside almost every building. Sometimes it was only a few dogs. Other times there were ten or more. Some of the dogs were just quietly sitting or lying down, but some were snarling or snapping or scrapping with each other, or barking greetings at us. The dogs *didn't* look friendly.

Commander Peary and the party stopped walking, and the men—at least a dozen of them—spread out in a circle around a small, smouldering fire. Everybody, with the exception of the Commander, sat down on the ground. Then Matt came forward and placed his bag on the ground by Peary.

Slowly, deliberately, Peary untied the bag. He reached in and pulled out . . . a metal pot? What was he doing with a pot? He held it over his head, like he was showing it off, and judging by the reaction of the Eskimos gathered around watching, it *had* impressed them. He placed the pot on the ground and reached into the bag again. This time he pulled out a knife—a long knife. He held it up, and the blade glittered as it caught the rays of the sun. There were more nods and smiles from the Eskimos. It *did* look like a nice knife. He placed it on the ground beside the pot. Next he pulled out a long, metal spearhead. This time the reaction was very noticeable. There was a general nodding of heads, smiles, and excited conversations broke out among the Eskimos.

"These are from me!" Peary proclaimed loudly. "For those men who come with me on this trip!"

Matt stepped forward and yelled out some words. I couldn't understand what he was saying. They were strange, hard-sounding words . . . it had to be Eskimo he was talking.

"I have more presents for all the men, women, and children who come with us!" Peary said.

Matt spoke—again in Eskimo talk—and people reacted with nods and smiles.

It was obvious what was going on. Matt was translating what the Commander was saying. But why didn't Commander Peary just say it himself? Unless he couldn't speak their language, and Matt could.

"We will be going north," Commander Peary said. "But not just north . . . we will be going so far north that there will only be one direction left to travel . . . south."

Matt translated his words, and the Eskimos reacted. Some laughed, a few shook their heads, and a few—the younger men—actually stood up and nodded excitedly in agreement.

"You know that I know every Eskimo from Cape York to Etah," Commander Peary said. "And of all those people, I have come to you, because I know the people of Etah are brave and strong, and that when others would turn back, they do not know fear."

Matt repeated his words. The excitement of a few seconds ago was replaced by looks of calm confidence, as if they maybe wouldn't say such a thing themselves, but it was an obvious truth.

"Over the next two days I will talk to people and select those who will come with us on our expedition. Thank you."

Once more Matt translated. I expected some sort of cheering or something. Instead, they slowly got to their feet and started to wander off, talking amongst themselves.

Peary walked over and put his arm around one of the Eskimos, and then the two of them walked off together, trailed by the four members of the expedition. The older Eskimo pulled aside a skin curtain that hung over the doorway to one of the stone homes and ushered the men inside. Then he followed, letting the curtain swing shut.

I looked over at Matt, who was putting the things back into the bag.

"Stay with me," he said.

No argument from me. He wouldn't be leaving my sight, even if he tried!

Chapter Six

AFTER MATT HAD FINISHED putting away the gifts for the Eskimos, he walked over to the building that the Commander and the rest of the men had disappeared into. He stopped by the skin door, gently placed the bag against the wall, and turned to walk away.

"Aren't we going in too?" I said.

He shook his head. "Nothing worth seeing is going to be happening in there. Come, I'll show you around and introduce you to some of my friends."

He started to walk and I fell in beside him.

"What *is* goin' to go on in there?" I asked.

"Sort of like a ceremony. The Commander is just going to exchange pleasantries with their leader—that older gentleman."

"Does their leader speak English?" I asked.

"Hardly any."

"Shouldn't you be in there to translate, then?"

"Commander Peary will do fine."

"Does he speak Eskimo?"

"Inuktitut is what it's called," Matt explained. "Yes, he speaks some."

"Then why did ya have to translate for 'im?"

"He speaks *some*. One or two words, mostly names of objects or orders."

"But you speak it really well . . . right?"

"I don't know if *really well* would be right. I don't know the words for a lot of things, and they tell me I say some words funny."

"But if you and the Commander have both been up here the same length of time, shouldn't he speak it as well as you do?" I asked.

"He's a very bright man," Matt said, "so I'm sure he could learn more if he felt the need. It's just that he has enough command of the language to make his wishes known."

"So why did *you* want to learn more?"

"You have a lot of questions," Matt said.

"Sorry, sir," I apologized, afraid that I had offended him.

"Don't apologize. I like that. Asking questions is how you learn about anything, and *why* I learned the language. How could I learn about these people and their lives if I couldn't speak their language?"

Three people—a man, woman, and child—came up to us, smiling, laughing. The man and Matt hugged. He then hugged the woman as well, and finally picked up the child and tossed him playfully into the air.

As they talked, my attention was caught by the dogs, a dozen or more on leather leads pegged to the ground. They were beautiful animals. Long silver-and-black coats and blue eyes! The dogs had blue eyes! Some of them were curled up together, sleeping. Two were having a tug-of-war with a bone. One dog stood, straining at his lead, his tail wagging, staring right at me with those beautiful blue eyes. He was tied up by himself, off to the side, and was probably lonely. I reached into my pants pocket and pulled out a piece of biscuit. He'd like that. I edged over closer and extended my hand toward him and—

"Danny!" Matt screamed, and I spun around. "What are you doing?"

I showed him the little piece of biscuit. "I was just goin' to give the dog a little treat, that's all."

"Toss it to him."

I lobbed the biscuit to the dog and he grabbed it, his jaws snapping together loudly.

"If you want to keep those fingers, you'd better keep them away from the dogs."

Instinctively I backed off a half-step, even though I was well out of reach.

"These aren't pets."

"But he looks friendly," I said, trying to defend myself.

"Some of them *are* friendly. Others aren't. You notice how that dog is tied off by itself?"

I nodded.

"It's probably not with the other dogs because it *isn't* so friendly. Sledge dogs can be unpredictable and wild. Come, I want you to meet these people."

I walked back over to join Matt. He introduced me, telling them my name and saying theirs. The names were strange-sounding and I knew I'd never be able to remember them.

While I couldn't understand the words that they were speaking, one thing was easy to understand: Matt was genuinely liked by these people, and he seemed to like them back. He gave them each a second hug and then we walked away.

"Everybody is very friendly," I said.

"Most hospitable people in the world. It feels good to be amongst them again. I've missed their kind souls. If you want, I could help teach you to speak Inuktitut."

"Would you?"

"We can start right now. Here's your first word. Say *ai*."

"*Ai*."

"Good. Say it again."

"*Ai*."

Matt smiled. "Now say that to them," he said, as two men came walking toward us.

"But . . . what does it mean?" I questioned.

"It means hello. Go ahead."

I turned around and looked at the men who continued to walk toward us. I felt nervous but I had to try. "*Ai*," I called out, and I waved, too, just in case I'd said it wrong.

They both burst into big smiles and waved and started talking excitedly. Of course I had no idea what they were talking about. Matt gave them both a pat on the back and they walked away.

"Do you see how happy they are when you make an effort to speak their language?"

"I was wondering," I said. "I keep hearing people say something when they see you."

He gave me a confused look.

"It sounds sort of like *maktak kabla* or something like that," I said.

Matt's face lit up and he laughed. "You mean *maktak kabloona*."

"That's it. What does that mean?"

He smiled. "It means black white man. They see me as being from away, a white man, but they can clearly see that I'm black." He paused. "I'm impressed you could pick that out. You have a very good ear for languages, so I'm sure you'll learn to speak Inuktitut very quickly. And you'll have many people to help you."

"How many Eskimos are coming with us?" I asked.

Matt shook his head. "Not sure. Could be forty."

"Forty!" I exclaimed. "Why so many?"

"It will take that many men if our mission is going to be successful. Do you know about the Peary system?"

I shook my head.

"It was created by the Commander. It involves the use of a number of different teams. Some teams lead, breaking trail, travelling light, while others follow, bringing supplies and caching them along the route. It takes a lot of men and a lot of dog teams."

"Dogs? I didn't know we was bringin' dogs with us."

"The Pole can't be reached without dogs," Matt explained. "Earlier Arctic explorers didn't realize that. The Commander learned many things from the Native peoples—the use of dogs, dressing in skins, living off the land whenever possible, and the use of Eskimo sledges— they called them komatiks. That could be your second word in Inuktitut. Say *komatik*."

"Komatik."

"You'll be talking like an Eskimo in no time. You'll have plenty of time—the whole winter to learn." Matt paused. "I was wondering, how old are you, Danny?"

"Fourteen."

"That makes you two years older than I was when I left home."

"You left when you were twelve?" That seemed so young.

"Not much choice. There really wasn't much to leave behind after my father died."

I felt my heart rise up into my throat.

"What's wrong?" Matt asked.

"My father died when I was seven," I said softly. "His ship went down and the whole crew was lost."

"What a tragedy. Your mother must have been devastated."

I nodded. "She was. Don't think she ever was the same again."

"Thank goodness you have your mother."

"Had," I said softly. "She died when I was the age you were when your father died." I felt myself starting to tear up. This was silly . . . it was over two years ago.

Matt put a hand on my shoulder. "Danny, *my* mother died when I was seven. You and I are like twins—we went through the same experiences, in different places and at different times. That makes us more alike than anybody else would know."

I looked up at Matt. His eyes had that sad, sorry, misty look that I was feeling.

"Hard stuff," Matt said. "When things get difficult, I try to remember the words of Friedrich Nietzsche."

"Is he a friend of yours?" I asked.

Matt smiled. "I guess he is, although I've only met him through his words and writing. He was a German philosopher. He said, 'What does not destroy me, makes me

stronger.'" He paused. "You and I, Danny, we survived the
deaths of our parents at a young age. It is tragic, but it has
made us both who we are. We are survivors, and to survive
we had to be strong."

"Sometimes I don't feel so strong," I said, my voice
cracking over the last words.

He put both hands on my shoulders and looked me
square in the eyes. "You *are* strong," he said.

Chapter Seven

August 28, 1908

THE SMOKE STREAMED OUT of the stacks as the engines worked hard to break through the layer of ice. The whole ship shuddered and for a split second was suspended in place before it crashed through and into open water. I shielded my eyes to try to follow the open lead—a little river of water cutting through the ice. It wasn't wide but it looked to extend for at least a mile or more. Good.

A few days' sailing north of Etah, the ocean ice had started to become almost a continuous sheet layering the ocean. The *Roosevelt* was strong and built to take on the ice, so the Captain had rammed his way through when it was thin enough. Other times the ice had rafted together and he'd had to move around it instead. We had shifted back and forth, like a drunken sailor, unable to move in a straight line. At times we'd been so firmly stuck in the ice that we didn't move at all—we were locked in place. When that happened, the Captain had to back his way out and look for another way through.

I'd heard grumblings from some of the sailors that they thought we weren't going to be able to make it to

Cape Sheridan. I didn't have any doubts. I knew that Captain Bartlett had done it before with this same ship, so why shouldn't he be able to do it again? If any man could do it, it was him. I figured if worst came to worst Captain Bartlett would climb out and walk along the ice, towing the boat behind him. I thought even the ice might be at least a little afraid of him and would get out of his way when he yelled. After all, there wasn't a man aboard, including Commander Peary, who didn't give the Captain a wide berth when he was angry about something.

Sometimes people did go out on the ice. They used axes and gigantic metal pry bars to chop and hack and create a little channel of open water for us to force our way through. Once, they even resorted to using a dynamite charge to blow up a place where the ice had rafted together and was too thick to chop through. There was a tremendous explosion and pieces of ice rained down from the sky.

I hadn't seen much of the Captain since we'd left Etah, ten days ago, but I'd certainly heard him. He was practically living up in the crow's nest, scouting out the best route, scouring the horizon, looking for little seams of open water or places where the ice wasn't as thick. Angus had explained to me that newly formed ice was a different colour—or actually a different *tint,* more blue than white. I couldn't really see that much of a difference but the experienced sailors could—especially Captain Bartlett. He could just tell.

"Danny!" Angus yelled out. He was holding two shovels. "Give us a 'and, mate."

I ran over and grabbed the second shovel. I had expected I might have lots of different duties on this trip, including shovelling snow. But I hadn't expected to be shovelling what I knew I was about to be shovelling. I followed Angus to the aft deck, which was entirely filled with dogs—two hundred and twenty-six sledge dogs. There was practically no spot on the deck that wasn't filled with a dog—or dog crap. That was what the shovels were for. We had to continually push it overboard. Angus said if we didn't he figured the weight of it would capsize the boat. I knew he was kidding me, but it was still amazing how much there was.

"Quite the stink, ain't it, boy?" Angus said.

"Worst thing I ever done smelled."

"Can ya imagine how much worse it would be if we wasn't doin' this a few times a day?" he said.

"Don't want to imagine that."

"I'll start toward the front an' you starts at the back, boy," Angus ordered.

I nodded and carefully tried to wind my way through the crowd of dogs. I didn't want to be stepping on anything I shouldn't, but my bigger fear was coming too close to one of the bad-tempered dogs. There had been more than one person bitten, and I'd had a couple of close calls myself, including having one dog rip a piece out of the seat of my pants. Thank goodness it hadn't ripped a piece out of *my* seat!

At first the dogs had all looked pretty much the same to me, but now I could tell many of them apart. I certainly knew the ones that were to be avoided, and which ones were gentle and friendly. I'd taken to bringing out extra scraps from the galley and feeding the nice ones.

As bad as the smell was, the noise was almost as terrible. The dogs could bark up a storm. And there always seemed to be one or two of them snarling or yelping or snapping at the others.

The funniest thing I ever saw involved the dogs and a big seal. The seal had heard the dogs barking and kept following after the ship, barking out his own challenge. The dogs closest to that side of the ship leaned over the railing and barked back. I think a couple would have jumped overboard if they hadn't been tied up. The racket went on for close to an hour before one of the crew got out a gun and took a shot at the seal. He didn't hit it, but the seal got the message and swam off.

I pushed a big shovelful of crap off the side of the boat and it disappeared into the foamy, greenish water. This was not the job I wanted to be doing. Up above, in the rigging, members of the crew were moving around like a bunch of spider monkeys, adjusting the sails to try to capture more of the wind. We needed the steam engines *and* the sails to give us enough power to break through the ice. Ever since first going up there to bring the Captain his supper that time, I'd gone up a dozen more times. I still couldn't move with the skill or confidence of the rest of the crew, but I was getting more comfortable, and if I wanted to be a sailor then I had to learn.

Off to my left, Ellesmere Island loomed large and ominous. It seemed to be nothing more than high cliffs and barren rock. I'm sure there was more, but from the ship I couldn't see life—not plant or animal. We'd been paralleling the shore for the last three days. There was a small lead—in many places narrower than the ship—that seemed to be following the shore. Angus had explained that this was the spot where the meltwater from the island met the ice and formed a river through the freezing ocean. I didn't know if that made sense, but I did know that it was the route we were travelling.

I used my shovel as a shield and a prod, forcing some of the dogs to move out of my way as I continued to work. One of the dogs I liked—I called him Blackie—wagged his tail at me but didn't move. I reached into my pocket and rummaged around for a treat. I found a little piece of biscuit.

"Sit!" I ordered.

Blackie cocked his head to the side, looking at me like he was trying to figure out what I was asking for.

"Better speak to 'im in Eskimo talk if ya wants 'im ta listen ta ya," Angus said.

"Maybe that's the next word I should learn."

"Maybe what we should do is stop feedin' 'em. If they don't eat, they can't crap," Angus suggested cheerfully.

"I don't think this little bit will matter," I said. I tossed the biscuit into the air and Blackie jumped up and caught it, his jaws coming together with an ominous snap. Nice or not, I wasn't putting my fingers too close.

Bit by bit, together, Angus and I finished clearing off the deck. It was still slippery and smelly and disgusting, but certainly a lot better than it had been before we started. We secured the shovels to the back wall of the aft cabin. I wanted to go and rinse off my boots, and maybe have a hot chocolate in the galley to try to wash the taste out of my mouth.

As I rounded the aft cabin I caught sight of Matt standing by the rail. I walked over to join him, wondering what he was watching. Without me asking, he pointed out to the ocean.

"Whales," he said.

"Where?"

"Watch that open patch of water off to starboard."

I scanned the ice until I located the lead. It was a long gash of green water amongst the white ice, but I didn't see anything—and then three fins broke the surface! I saw a little wisp of steam rise up as they all exhaled.

"I see them!" I exclaimed.

"Keep your voice down," he warned me. "As long as nobody notices they're out there, then nobody will try to kill them."

I understood what he meant. It seemed like every time we passed a seal or a flock of birds or anything one of the expedition members would take a shot at it.

"People from the south see an animal and they think they should kill it," Matt said.

"Don't you hunt?" I asked.

"I hunt when I need to survive, just like the Eskimos. No shame in killing an animal to feed yourself or your family. I just don't see it as sport. You want to make it fair, then give the whale a gun so it can return fire. *That* would be sport."

I had to laugh. Matt made me laugh.

"An Eskimo kills a seal and he uses everything—meat, blubber, skin, bones—everything. I admire that. A white man takes a shot at some seal on the ice. Maybe he wounds it, maybe he kills it, but it slips back into the water and is gone." He shook his head. "Just a waste."

I guess I'd never thought of it that way before, but it sounded as though Matt had thought about it a lot.

"I see you're spending a lot of time with the huskies," he said.

"I don't have much choice. Somebody has to clean up the mess," I told him.

"Sure, but I've seen you down there patting the dogs, spending time with them even when you're not cleaning."

"I like dogs. Some of them are nice."

"Most people can't tell one husky from another. For them, all sledge dogs look the same," Matt said.

"But they're nothing alike. They're all different."

"How about our Eskimo guests?" Matt asked.

I shrugged. "I'm sure they can tell them apart."

Matt laughed. "I mean, can you tell the Eskimos apart, or do they all just look alike to you?"

"I can tell some of them apart," I said. I definitely could tell the men from the women and the children from the adults. And there were lots of them—forty-nine Eskimos. Twenty-two men, seventeen women, and ten children. I hadn't expected there to be women or children along, but they were all part of a large family group—brothers and sisters, uncles and cousins. I guess it made sense for whole families to come along. We were going to be gone for the better part of a year—maybe two if the ice locked us in—and it would be hard to be away from your family that long . . . the way I was always going to be away from my family.

I suddenly felt very sad and very alone.

"There's no point in me teaching you Inuktitut if you're not going to use it," Matt said. "Come, I want you to meet some more friends of mine."

I followed Matt and we made our way toward the fore-deck—away from the dogs and their stink, with a stiff, fresh breeze blowing into our faces.

All of the Eskimos were on the foredeck. They were *living* out there. There was space for them down below in the hole, but they didn't want to live below decks. They hardly ever even *went* inside.

Some of the children, including a couple who were about my age, were in a group playing a game. It was sort of like a game of dice, with the dice made out of animal bones. I'd been invited by the kids to play their games before, but I was always too busy with work. Besides, I didn't feel much like a kid.

A number of the women were sitting, sewing skins together. Some people were leaning against the railing, looking out at the water and ice. There were five men squatting in a little circle. I'd noticed how they often squatted, on their feet, legs bent, backs straight, balanced, rather than sitting. They were talking and smoking and talking.

"*Ai!*" Matt called out, and I said the same as they called out their greetings.

Two of them shuffled over to the side, creating a space in the circle. Matt squatted down to join them and motioned for me to do the same. I tried to squat down the same way everybody else did and almost lost my balance, nearly tumbling backwards before I settled in.

Matt said something and the men all chuckled. I guess he told them a joke—or were they all laughing at me almost falling over?

Matt spoke again and now the men nodded their heads in agreement.

"Learn Inuktitut . . . good boy," one of the Eskimos said as he reached out and tapped me on the leg.

"Thanks."

"You help?" Matt asked the man.

He nodded. "Help, yes." He turned to me. "Help Oatah learn English?"

I didn't understand what he meant.

"That is Oatah," Matt said. "He wants you to help him learn English and he'll help you to learn Inuktitut."

"Oh, yeah, sure," I said, nodding my head enthusiastically.

Matt said something else in Inuktitut and all five men smiled and nodded. The man beside me patted me on the back.

The ship suddenly shuddered to a stop and I almost tumbled over again. Matt reached out and grabbed me by the arm, stopping me from falling.

Obviously we'd hit a thicker piece of ice and . . . now there was no sound. All the time we moved we could hear the sound of the ship breaking through the ice. It was such a constant that I only noticed it now because it was gone. There was just silence. I couldn't hear the engines working, but I could feel them pulsing up through the deck, vibrating up into my body.

I stood up, as did everybody else, and we made our way to the railing. I looked over the side and toward the bow. The lead we had been following had vanished, replaced by a ridge of rafting ice and a sheet of solid ice stretching out to the horizon.

The still air was split open by Captain Bartlett, yelling from the crow's nest. His words were directions and orders, littered with a healthy dose of profanity. I figured even if the orders didn't succeed in freeing up the ship the swear words might melt a path in the ice.

"How far are we from Cape Sheridan?" I asked.

"No more than forty miles," Matt replied.

I was almost afraid to say what I was going to ask next because of what he might answer, but I really needed to know.

"The Cap'n can get through this, right?" I asked.

"If anybody can, he can. He might have to send out a crew to chop or pry or blast, but we're not done . . . at least, not yet."

"But he might not be able to get us all the way to the Cape?"

"He did it the last time. He pushed the ship to the limits, demanded almost more of her than was possible. Just hope he can do it again."

"Why wouldn't he be able to do it?"

Matt gestured with his arms. "The Arctic is wild and unpredictable and so massive that it makes any man seem small and insignificant and powerless. Even a man like Captain Bartlett or Commander Peary. If this can be done, those men will do it. I just don't know if it can be done."

Chapter Eight

September 5, 1908

I PULLED DOWN THE HOOD of my parka. Standing at the farthest point forward on the bow of the ship, I leaned over the railing. It was incredible to watch as the hull of the ship ate up the ice and churned it into splinters and shards and boulder-sized chunks, while greenish-blue water sloshed over the surface and smoothed our passage. I knew the ice couldn't be very thick—not just because we were able to push through it, but because of the look of it. I could tell by the tint of the ice if it was thick or thin.

Oatah had taught me about the ice. He'd been teaching me a lot of things. When I wasn't on duty or sleeping I'd spent all of the last few days up on the deck with him. Oatah was always trying to explain things to me, gesturing and pointing, using words that I didn't understand to describe things that I often couldn't even see. He'd be gesturing excitedly, pointing into the distance, and all I could see was ice. Then, if I was patient, as we got closer to the object, or the object got closer to us, I could make things out. Sometimes it was birds flying just above the horizon, or seals on the ice, or once, a big polar bear lumbering along the ice.

I'd learned to trust his eyes. Maybe I'd learned to trust mine more, too. I was seeing things more clearly, more quickly, noticing little differences that I hadn't noticed before.

Captain Bartlett screamed down an order from the crow's nest for the ship to come to, and within seconds it tilted to one side and followed his direction. I had the strangest thought that it wasn't anybody steering or responding to his order but the ship itself simply listening and doing what it was told.

For the first time since we'd left the Etah Fjord, there was land on both sides of us. We were working our way deeper into a bay, a harbour, where the ship would be spending the winter. This was the same place they had wintered before—the farthest north that any ship had ever travelled. Captain Bartlett had done it!

There were times when I'd had my doubts. Over the past five days we'd been stopped repeatedly. We'd doubled back, tried new routes, sent men out with axes and pry bars and dynamite. One day we'd barely travelled ten miles. And I was told that the day before we'd sailed almost twenty miles but only gone three miles north.

I looked out at the coast. It was rough, rocky, and barren. If there was life to be seen it wasn't going to be from this distance with the naked eye. I pulled up the binoculars that hung around my neck. George had lent them to me. They were hard to focus, but I worked until I had a better look at the shore. The rocks and ruggedness were still visible, but I could also see what looked like grass—probably muskeg—and patches of colour . . . flowers.

I caught sight of movement against a cliff. It was small and fleeting, and then I focused. It was birds. Dozens—no, there were *hundreds,* maybe *thousands* of birds flying up and down and around the cliff face. They had to be nesting. Amazing. This wasn't just ice and snow and rock. Even up here, farther north than any man could live, life existed. Birds and flowers, seals and polar bears, and, of course, all the things that lived beneath the surface of the ocean and the ice.

"See anything interesting?"

I put down the binoculars. It was Matt.

"I see nothin' that *isn't* interestin'."

Matt smiled. "That is a very good answer. Are you going to be happy to be on solid land?"

"I will be, but not as happy as the Eskimos."

"You're right about that. They don't seem to like being cooped up on a ship. I can't say I won't be glad to get the dogs off, as well."

"Think how I feel!" I said. "You're not the one cleanin' up after 'em. Will we be landing today?"

He nodded. "As soon as we drop anchor, everybody will be put to work to set up a camp on shore."

"I thought we'd be staying on the ship . . . living onboard."

"Some people will stay on the ship, but it's important to get everything that's needed off the ship as quickly as possible. You can never tell about the ice."

"But . . . but we're here . . . we don't have to worry about the ice now," I said.

"We always have to worry about the ice. Whether we're moving or not, the ice is always moving. Depending on the winds and currents, the ice can raft, pick the ship up, rip open a hole in the bottom, or tip it onto its side."

How could that be?

"Last trip here, the ship was caught in shifting ice and tilted up close to forty-five degrees," Matt said, holding his arm out to show the angle of the ship. "Then, just as it looked like the *Roosevelt* was going to be lost, the ice opened, released the ship, and she settled back down into the water."

"If that happened, if the ship was lost, how would we get back home?"

"You've been tending to the answer," Matt said. "Dog teams and sledges would take us down Ellesmere and eventually back to Etah."

"That sounds simple enough," I said.

"Simple, but not easy. It would be very difficult, especially if we didn't have enough dogs. How are the dogs?"

"Another one died yesterday." It was a big, white-faced male dog. He'd been getting sicker and sicker, losing it through both ends for the past few days, throwing up and getting the runs. I couldn't help picturing the dead dog being thrown overboard. I knew there really wasn't another way to do it—it wasn't like they could bury it—but it still struck me as harsh. What would we do if a person died? No, we wouldn't do *that*.

"How many dogs have died?" Matt asked.

"Fifteen."

"Thank goodness the Commander had the foresight to bring close to two hundred and fifty dogs along. We still have more than we need."

"We do, but there are more dogs that aren't well."

The sick dogs were throwing up and had the runs, making the mess on the deck even worse.

"How many more dogs are affected?" Matt asked.

"At least as many again."

"We still have enough. The dogs will do better once we're on shore, once we can separate them. Getting the healthy dogs away from the sick ones can only be a good thing."

"I hope so."

"Now, there's still time to get some grub before we drop anchor. You hungry?"

"I think I could eat a bite or two," I said, with a grin.

I TENTATIVELY PUT one foot down on the ice, and then the other. This was silly. I knew it could hold me, like it was already holding the dozens of men and dogs and sledges and crates that were already on the ice.

Matt had, of course, been right. No time was wasted. Within thirty minutes of dropping anchor they had started to unload the ship. Between my shipboard tasks—including scrubbing and cleaning the deck after the dogs had been brought down to the ice—I'd been watching. The first men, driving a team of dogs, their sledges loaded with equipment, had started off across the ice toward land.

The *Roosevelt* now sat in the middle of a solid sea of ice. The path that we'd broken to get here had refrozen. The ice had a different hue, and I could still see the path we'd travelled, but there was no more open water. The ship was locked in place. Funny, the last thing I'd wanted for the past few weeks was for the ice to be solid. Now, as

I was standing on the surface, I wanted it to be as thick as possible.

There was a strong wind, whipping up snow and blowing it almost horizontally across the ice. I pulled the hood of my parka tighter around my head and moved over until I was shielded from the wind by a pile of wooden crates stacked to form a protective wall.

There was a blur of activity all around. All of the dogs that weren't being used to ferry supplies to shore were pegged down on the ice. Being off the ship seemed to agree with them as they looked frisky, as though they were happy to be on solid land . . . solid ice.

Equally happy were the Eskimos. I didn't think they liked being confined to the ship any more than the dogs did. They were working, but there was laughter, and it seemed like everybody was smiling. They must have felt like they were home. I knew they were far from Etah, but this was a lot more like what they were used to than being penned up on a ship.

Me, I liked the ship. I enjoyed sitting in the galley, at the big table, sipping a cup of tea or coffee and talking to Cookie. I liked being up on the deck. I was feeling a lot more comfortable in the rigging. Heck, I even liked the little section of the sleeping quarters I shared with five other crew, including Angus, who could snore so loud that it drowned out the noise of the ice against the hull.

I looked around for Matt, or the Commander, or any member of the expedition. None were here. They'd all probably gone in with the first sledges—the first komatiks—to start setting things up. The Captain and all the rest of the crew were still onboard.

As I stood there, I saw a team pulling a komatik coming back toward us. As it got closer, the barking of the dogs got the rest of our dogs excited and they joined in. It sounded as if they were cheering them on. I wondered who was driving the team. It would be best if it was the Commander. If it was, I could ask him if I could go along, drive in with a team and go to land. I wanted land under my feet. Of course, that was only part of it. I was just plain curious, and I wanted to know where they were making camp and what it looked like.

"Ya cold, Danny?"

I turned around. It was the Captain.

"A little, I guess, sir."

"Gonna get a whole lot colder before this is over. Remember, this is summer."

I laughed. "Not like any summer I've seen before."

"So what are ya doin' down 'ere?" he asked.

"Just watchin'."

"Ya can learn a lot, just by lookin'. You're a curious sort of lad," he said. "Just remember, curiosity killed the cat."

"I'll be careful, sir. Just lookin', that's all."

"Do ya want ta do more than just look?" Captain Bartlett asked.

I didn't know what he meant. Was he was trying to trick me or—

"I'm goin' to shore. Do ya want to come along?" he asked.

"Could I?"

"Wouldn't ask if I didn't mean it." He paused. "Besides, probably the best way to keep ya safe is to keep one eye on ya. Let me pick out the dogs and—"

"Could I pick the dogs, sir?" I asked.

"You?"

"I've spent a lot of time with them, you know, cleanin' up and such," I explained. "I know 'em real well."

"Knowin' 'em an' knowin' which ones will work as a team are two different things," Captain Bartlett said. "But . . . go ahead, give it a whirl."

Chapter Nine

I'D PICKED OUT THE DOGS, one by one. The Captain hooked up the first two and then showed me how to hook the third up to the line. With the fourth dog I did it myself. He checked the lead, making sure I'd tied it the way he'd shown me. He didn't say anything, but then he didn't check the rest after that, so I must have done it right.

The dogs were being tied together in a sort of fan pattern, two dogs together, each pair on a separate lead, angling away from the sledge. That was different from what I'd expected or seen back at Etah.

"How come they're not being tied together in a straight line?" I asked Captain Bartlett.

"You questionin' how I'm doin' things?" he asked.

"No, sir!" I exclaimed, practically saluting him.

He smiled, and I realized he was just joking with me again.

"On solid land you tie them straight, best way to get the most power pulling forward," he said. "Can't do that on the ice. If the lead dog broke through the ice the whole team would go through into the water, maybe drown the lot, maybe even take the sledge and driver with them."

A chill went up my spine and I suddenly didn't feel so safe standing on the ice.

"By tyin' 'em this way, in a fan pattern, only a couple might go in and the rest would stay on top, pullin' the stragglers out. Make sense?" he asked.

"Yes, sir." I hesitated before asking the next question, but I wanted to know. "Is there any danger of *us* fallin' in?"

"Always a danger."

That wasn't the answer I'd been hoping for, and I started worrying that the ice under my feet wasn't as thick as I'd thought.

"You just stay close to me, an' if anythin' bad happens I'll take care of it. Ever fallen through ice before?"

"No," I said, shaking my head. "I was sort of hopin' to keep it that way."

"Not much chance of that."

Again, not the answer I'd wanted to hear.

"First time is the worst," he said. "Important thing to remember is not to panic. Just close your mouth and wait to pop to the surface. We'll get ya out."

Instinctively I closed my mouth and nodded my head.

"Scared?"

"Should I be?" I asked.

"Not today. Pretty thick," he said, and he stomped his heel against the ice.

That was the first thing he'd said that made me feel better.

" . . . At least 'ere. Close to shore might be tricky."

So much for feeling better.

"Go and get the last dog," he ordered.

"Yes, sir."

I walked very slowly across the ice, wondering if each step might be the one that put me through the ice.

I selected the final dog—the tenth dog—and tied him into place.

I had been careful with each dog I'd picked. I wanted animals that wouldn't bite me or any of the other dogs. These were the nicest dogs—and I knew the dogs better than maybe anybody except the Eskimos. Some of the dogs—often the biggest, strongest males—were nasty. I had avoided those ones. I wanted the dogs that wouldn't cause me any problems.

All the time I'd been choosing the dogs, others had been working to load the sledge. One of the big wooden crates had been placed on it and then other objects had been tied onto the top.

"Nice-lookin' team, Danny," Captain Bartlett said. "Couple of those dogs are small. Not the most powerful, but then we're not goin' far. Now, come, I'm gonna show ya how to drive 'em."

I followed him to the back of the sledge.

"You and me are gonna take turns runnin' and ridin'. When you're ridin', you put your hands here," he said, pointing to two handles that extended at the back of the komatik. "Ya have to take this lead," he said, grabbing a long piece of rawhide that led over the sledge and was connected to the leashes of all the dogs. "And ya put your feet on these runners," he said, pointing down. "Actually, put one foot on the runner an' push with the other, like this."

He grabbed the handles, holding the lead with his right hand, and put his left foot on the runner. With his right foot he pushed against the ice.

"Like that. Okay?"

"I can try."

"Good, 'cause it's time to give it a whirl."

Now I didn't feel so sure or so brave. He handed me the lead. I grabbed the handle with one hand and placed one foot on the runner, and stood there, waiting.

The Captain walked around the sledge to the dogs. Three were lying down, fanned out in front. He gave the lead dog a poke with the side of his boot and it jumped up. The others realized something was happening and got to their feet. He grabbed the line of the lead dog, yelled out something in Inuktitut, and pulled the dog forward. The whole team responded, and if I hadn't been holding on I might have tumbled over as the sledge surged forward.

The sledge started moving slowly. Still holding on to the handles and the lead, I jumped off to lessen the weight. The sledge started to move faster so I put one foot back on the runner and pushed with the other. This wasn't so hard. It was sort of fun.

Captain Bartlett was now running beside the sledge rather than in front of it. The sledge wasn't moving very fast but I had to wonder how long the Captain could keep up this pace. He wasn't a young man—he must have been in his thirties.

"Cap'n . . . I can run," I yelled out.

"Not yet."

I kept my foot on the runner and kept pushing.

I was holding onto the lead but I realized that I didn't actually know how to drive the dogs, or stop them, or steer them. I was at the back of the sledge but I wasn't much more than baggage. How did the dogs even know which way to go? They were going the right way, weren't they? They had to be, or the Captain would have stopped them.

I looked up ahead, looking for something on shore to steer toward, or a path that had been scored by the previous teams. I couldn't see anything, and the ice was hard and clean and unmarked. There was nothing . . . Wait. Up ahead I saw something dark on the ice. Was it a seal? Whatever it was we were headed straight for it. I expected it to move, run away, but instead it just stayed there, getting bigger and bigger. As we got closer it stayed put. What sort of animal would just sit there as we came charging toward it? Even if it were blind it couldn't have helped but notice the continual barking and yelping of the dogs. It couldn't be an animal, it couldn't be anything alive.

There was also something about the colour—maybe it was the ice playing tricks on my eyes but it looked bluish and . . . then it came to me. It was a metal container, one of the gigantic metal cans that held pemmican. It was on its side, standing almost a foot and a half wide and three feet high. How did that get out here? Maybe it fell off one of the other sledges . . . but why was it standing on its side like that?

"Cap'n!" I yelled. "Up ahead . . . do ya see it?"

"'Course I see it!" he called back. "That's one of the markers!"

Markers . . . that made perfect sense. That explained how we could find our way across the ice. But, how did the dogs know this was the way?

As we got closer to the marker the Captain moved to the front of the team. He grabbed the lead and yanked the dog off to the side, and the whole team and sledge followed after it. That was how the dogs knew where to go, because the Captain knew where to go.

I looked ahead, starting right in front and then allowing my eyes to move forward, slowly, toward the horizon. That was the way Oatah had shown me. There was nothing close at hand. I tried to trace the path directly in front of us, the route we were headed on. There, way up ahead, I could see a dark shape. It glistened slightly in the sun—the way a large metal container would—and I knew where we were going.

"Off!" Captain Bartlett yelled.

For a split second I didn't react, and then I realized. Captain Bartlett reached out and grabbed the lead from me. I let go of the handles and jumped off to one side, almost falling over as I hit the ice. The sledge surged forward and I scrambled, trying to catch up. I got level with the sledge and then slowed down so I could match the pace of the dogs.

As we kept moving I was starting to feel the strain in my legs and lungs. I was drawing in gigantic lungfuls of air and the cold etched a line down my throat and into my chest. My legs were aching and getting heavier and heavier. I wanted to stop, but I knew I couldn't. I kept going, step after step. I tried to get my mind off of the ice and onto the shore ahead. I knew it was getting closer with each step but it still wasn't close. If I could get there the camp probably wouldn't be too far. I really wanted to get ashore, away from any danger of falling through the ice. It was funny, though—if what the Captain had said was true, and the ice got more dangerous

closer to shore, the closer I got to safety the more dangerous it would get.

We were now close enough for me to have a good idea
where we were going. There was a low, flat spot—I
guessed it to be some sort of beach—that was bordered on
both sides by higher, dark, rocky cliffs. Then, as confir-
mation, I caught sight of the glittering metal of one of the
pemmican cans on the shore.

Our pace seemed to quicken the closer we got to the
beach. It seemed like the dogs were getting more excited.
Their barking got louder and more frequent and . . . no,
that wasn't it. I was just hearing their yelps and barks
bouncing back off the cliffs that were looming ever closer,
and—

"Aaaahhhh!" I screamed as my legs crashed through
the ice! A bolt of freezing water surged through my legs
as they plummeted below the ice! My momentum
pushed me forward and my body slammed down and
then broke through, throwing the rest of me into the
water. Desperately I clawed at the ice, trying to pull
myself forward. It crumbled away in my fingers and
I couldn't get a grip! I was going down . . . I was going
to go under . . . I was going to drown!

Chapter Ten

"HELP!" I SCREAMED as I struggled to keep my head and shoulders above the water.

I looked up. Bartlett and the team had stopped—thank God—and the Captain was standing there, staring at me . . . but he wasn't coming back to help.

I kept clawing at the ice and it kept giving way and—

"Stand up!" Bartlett yelled.

What was he talking about?

"Stand up!" he yelled.

My feet sank down to the bottom. The water was only two or three feet deep. I stood there, in waist-deep water, feeling even more stupid than cold.

"You plannin' on stayin' in there all day?" Captain Bartlett called out.

I tried to climb out and onto the ice but it kept giving way under my weight, and I stumbled, almost toppling over before finally securing a solid footing. I sloshed over toward the Captain, my clothing, soaked, weighing me down.

"Strange place to take a bath," Captain Bartlett said. "Once we get to the camp ya better get out of those clothes and into somethin' dry."

"Is it far?" I asked. The temperature was warm—a few degrees above freezing—but the wind was strong and I felt shivers already radiating throughout my body.

"Not far. Get on the komatik and I'll run alongside," the Captain said.

I took the lead as the Captain went to the front of the pack. The dogs had all settled down and were sitting or lying on the ice. He yanked the front pair to their feet and then dragged them forward, yelling out something. The dogs all jumped up and started moving. This time I was ready for the surge forward and held on tightly.

The dogs gained speed and I slid along with them, pushing with one foot, resting the other on the skid. We started to move up an incline—a sure sign that we were finally off the ice and onto the ice-covered land. Straight ahead I spotted another one of the pemmican cans, marking the way. The path continued to rise and then, after hitting that marker, cut sharply to the right, slicing between two cliffs. We were in a little valley and there were high walls of rock on both sides. I looked way up. There were little pockets of ice and snow, but it was almost all brown and bare, the only white coming from the birds that were clinging to the rock face.

The trail snaked along between the cliffs. In places it wasn't very wide, and the dogs had to cluster together to get through the opening. Looking farther forward, though, I could see that it was opening up, getting wider and wider . . . and green. There was snow on the one side, the side protected from the sun by the rocks, but on the other side the ground was green—things were growing! That only made sense, it was still only September, so this was probably the last breath of life before the winter would swallow things up again. Just like this was the only time of the year that the birds could migrate this far north and survive before they retreated back south again.

The river of snow we were travelling on was getting narrower and narrower and I could now see that the green ahead was a combination of grass and muskeg, and scattered amongst it were flowers—dozens and dozens of red and yellow flowers. They looked so small, so delicate. Somehow they'd survived the bitter winter and burst into life again when the good weather allowed. That was amazing—and encouraging. We were going to be here for the bitter winter, surviving, and then coming to life in the spring when the weather allowed. If a bunch of little flowers could do it, we could do it too.

Up ahead I saw the camp. Well, at least what would become the camp. There were three teams of dogs resting, a dozen men, and a whole cluster of crates that had already been removed from the ship. They were piled together. The snow cover was even more sparse and we hit a patch of gravel and grass, the sledge slowing down before the dogs powered us over it. Finally, the Captain yelled out an order and the dogs slowed down, came to a stop, and then dropped to the ground amongst the other huskies and sledges.

"Welcome home," Captain Bartlett said. "Not much yet, but the view is outta this world."

"This is home?" I asked.

"It will be, at least for a little while. Beautiful, isn't it?"

I nodded. It was.

"Feast your eyes on the colours while you can. Soon there'll be no more greens or blues or yellows or reds. All will be white or shades of white. The closest you'll see to colour is the blue tinge in the ice."

"How soon before the snows come?"

"It's already snowed here a few times, but melted."

"How soon before it doesn't melt?" I asked.

"Could be anytime." He looked up at the sky, studying it. I knew he could read the sky the way other people could read a book. "But not tonight."

I bent down and picked one of the little flowers. It was a beautiful bright blue, small, fragile. It felt as though it might crumble in my hand, so I held it delicately.

"It's pretty amazing that something like this could survive up here all winter and then bloom in the spring," I said.

"Amazing and inspiring. That's what we're gonna try to do."

"But we're not a flower," I said, holding it up.

"That we're not. The flower has an advantage over us."

I gave him a questioning look.

"That flower *belongs* here."

"And we don't?"

"No, sir. Even the Eskimos, the people of the north, don't come up this far."

"But we're here now."

"Being here doesn't mean that we belong here. We're just strangers in a strange land. Next spring the flowers will bloom again . . . Us . . . time will tell."

A shiver went up my spine that had nothing to do with my wet clothing and the wind.

The Captain chuckled. "Don't you go worryin' none. We'll survive. Now, if *you're* going to survive to even see winter, we'd better get you some dry clothing."

He untied the rope holding down the supplies on the sledge. He took down a cloth bag and passed it to me. It was surprisingly heavy. He motioned for me to take a second sack and I dropped the first to the ground. It landed with a thud, and then there was the unmistakable tinkling of metal against metal.

"You'll find some dry clothing in this sack," he said as he handed it to me. "Change."

"Here?" I asked.

He looked around. "For somebody who took a bath in the ocean I wouldn't be thinkin' you'd need much privacy. You 'aven't got nothin' that everybody hasn't seen before. I'm heading down to the campsite. Change, then take a hammer and spike out of that first bag and stake the dogs in place. After that you can come and join us. Lots of work to be done."

I waited until the Captain had started to walk away and then looked around. There were a bunch of people at the camp—maybe a dozen or more Eskimos, as well as Dr. Goodwill, Mr. Marvin, Mr. MacMillan, and George. Commander Peary was nowhere to be seen, and none of the Eskimos were women. I guessed it was okay to change.

I took partial cover behind the sledge, using it as a screen between me and the men at the campsite. First I kicked off my mukluks. They were sopping wet, and as I pulled off the second one I turned it over and a stream of water poured out. I took off my parka. It was wet on the outside, especially at the bottom, but the sealskin had held strong and the water hadn't penetrated through. I took it off and laid it on the sledge. My shirt was the same as the parka, just wet at the bottom, but I'd be best to put on a dry one. I took it off and dropped it to the ground. Next I pulled off my socks and pants. Any thought of leaving my underpants on vanished as I realized they were just as wet as everything else. I pulled them off as well and felt very, very exposed. The breeze made my skin tingle. I guessed that wasn't bad. The wind was going to have to dry me off before I put anything else on or there really wasn't much to be gained by changing.

I reached into the bag and rummaged around. There was a coat—sealskin—pants—sealskin as well—shirts, and a couple of pairs of mukluks. I searched around. No underpants. That sealskin was going to be pretty rough against my privates, but there didn't seem to be any real— I heard the barking of dogs and turned around. Another team was coming toward me—toward me standing there *buck naked*!

I grabbed the pants and pulled them on one leg, hopping on one foot until I could pull them onto my other leg. They were too short in the leg and too wide in the waist but they'd have to do. I grabbed a shirt and pulled it on over my head, tucking it into the pants. There was still too much room. I grabbed a second shirt and pulled it over, tucking it into my pants as well. The two shirts, bunched up, looked like they might keep the pants from falling down to my ankles.

I took a mukluk from the larger of the two pairs and shoved in my foot. It was a bit small, but small and dry was better than soaked and fitting. I pulled on the second and then grabbed my parka and threw it back on top just as the dog team pulled to a stop beside me. It was Oatah!

He gave me a questioning look. Obviously he had seen me getting dressed but didn't know what to make of it.

"I fell through the ice and had to change clothes," I said, pointing to the soaked clothing lying at my feet.

"Aahhh," he said, nodding in agreement.

I wanted to go down to the campsite but I had to spike down the dogs first. I grabbed the first bag, loosened the drawstrings, and looked inside. Right on top was a large wooden mallet. Beneath it were long metal spikes. I pulled out the mallet and one of the spikes.

Oatah looked over my shoulder. "Smart. Care for dogs and dogs care for you."

I was going to tell him it wasn't my idea, but I liked him thinking I was smart about some things. Since it always seemed like I was the student and he was the teacher, I felt like I must have looked pretty stupid most of the time. Things about the animals, and the ice, and of course the language, things that even little Eskimo kids knew, I didn't. Although I was learning.

"Do you want me to stake down your dogs after?" I asked.

He nodded.

I looped the harness of the lead dog around the stake. I pushed it into the ground. The first few inches went in effortlessly and then it came to a dead stop. It would have to be driven the rest of the way. I tapped the mallet against the head of the stake. It sank a little bit lower. I gave it another tap and it sank in lower. Then I hit it a third time and it didn't budge. The ground was a little more solid. I drew back the mallet and gave it a big smash. Vibrations shot back up through my arm and the stake hardly budged. It was like I had hit a big rock . . . then I remembered. No rock, just ground, solid, frozen ground. The earth, just a foot or so below the surface, was permanently frozen. Even in the middle of summer—if that's what you could call July up here—only the top layer of soil ever unfroze.

I took the mallet with both hands and drew it back over my head. I swung it down with all my might and the stake slipped in a couple more inches. I swung again and again, and slowly the stake went in until only the top five or six inches were showing. That would be solid enough to hold the team in place.

Oatah had been unloading his sledge and I walked over, taking another stake with me.

"Lots of stuff," I said.

He gave me a questioning look.

"Stuff, things, supplies . . . lots of things we'll need."

"Stuff." He had a large canvas bag slung over his shoulder and he started walking toward the campsite.

I went to grab the harness of his lead dog and it snarled and tried to bite me! Instinctively I jumped back, but at the same time I brought the stake down over the dog's head. The dog yelped and jumped back. I really didn't like hitting a dog, but I'd learned that with some of them you just had to. If they didn't know you were in charge of them, they thought they were in charge of you. The dog laid down on the ground, its tail wagging nervously. As I brought the mallet down on the spike the dog winced—it must have thought I was going to hit it again. That made me feel bad—but not as bad as being bitten. I finished banging the stake in and I was free to go down to the camp.

I started off and then skidded to a stop. There was no point in going down there empty-handed. I grabbed a box from the sledge and started down again.

The ground at the camp was littered with boxes and bags, things that had been brought off the ship. The men were all occupied moving the large wooden crates. I didn't like the crates. They reminded me of just one thing—coffins. They were just about the right size. They were stacking them on top of each other, four tall. Why would they do that? It wasn't like there wasn't enough space. It was an enormous empty field on a gigantic empty island. There wasn't anybody other than us around for thousands of miles.

That thought reverberated around in my head. The people of the *Roosevelt* were the only people for thousands and thousands of miles. We were going to be alone up here, isolated from the entire world by a thick layer of ice locking the ship in and the world out, covered by a layer of snow, battling temperatures that would be unbelievably, indescribably bitter, trying to survive the winter, waiting for spring to make a run for the Pole. What had I gotten myself into?

Chapter Eleven

September 21, 1908

I STOPPED AT THE DOOR of the Captain's cabin. I could hear music. I didn't know what it was but it was beautiful. Lush, full, beautiful. I raised my hand to knock but stopped myself. It didn't seem right to interrupt music as fine as that. It just didn't seem respectful. Maybe I should wait or come back later . . . but it would have to be a whole lot later. The Captain almost always had something playing on his gramophone.

Besides, it wasn't so much the music that was stopping me as the feeling in the pit of my stomach. Why had the Captain ordered me to leave the campsite and come to speak to him on the *Roosevelt,* in his cabin? What was it that he had to say to me that he didn't want to say in front of the other crew members? Was it about something that I'd done wrong? I knew I wasn't picking up all the lessons I was supposed to be learning about being a seaman but I was trying and—the music stopped.

I knocked.

"Enter!" the Captain's voice called through the closed door.

I opened it and peeked inside. "It's me, sir."

"Yes, yes, come in."

He was leaning over his gramophone. His back was to me.

"Take a seat, Danny," he said, gesturing to three chairs around a table. I went over and sat.

I watched as, with two hands, he removed the record. He returned it to a paper sleeve and then put that sleeve into another, leather sleeve. He handled the record delicately, like it was a baby. I guess it was pretty fragile.

"Bach," he said.

"Yes, always good ta put things back where they belong," I agreed.

He turned around with an amused look on his face. "Not *back,* Bach. This is a symphony composed by Johann Sebastian Bach."

"That name sounds familiar, it does."

"Born in Germany in 1685. He was an organist of great talent, but his legacy is as one of the greatest composers of all time."

"It sounded pretty," I said, "the little bit I heard through the door."

"Have you never heard his music before?" he asked.

I shook my head. "Mostly fiddle music where I come from."

"And in church . . . when you used to go to church?"

"Hymns and things mostly."

"Did your church not have an organ?" he asked.

I shook my head. "Not big enough."

"That's sad. Music, especially the power of the organ, can elevate and exalt the spirit of our Lord. If there had been an organ ya would 'ave heard some Bach. He wrote a lot of music for church. He was a church organist. Here, let me put on another of his symphonies."

As he looked through the record albums I looked around the room. Aside from the records and the gramophone, the most dominant things were the gigantic wooden desk, papers scattered about, and the walls—nothing but shelves filled with books. There were hundreds—no, thousands! I didn't think there were that many books anywhere in the world.

"I think this will appeal ta your ear," Captain Bartlett said.

He placed the record on the turntable and it started spinning around. Carefully, his eye level with it, he placed the arm of the gramophone down, the needle touching the disc with a soft, staticky sound. It hissed for a few seconds and then the sound of a whole orchestra came charging out of the gigantic bell of the gramophone. He fiddled with a dial on the front of the machine and the sound soared, filling the cabin! Captain Bartlett stood, his eyes closed, a joyful look on his face, and waved his arms gently in the air like he was some sort of conductor. Finally he reached out and turned that same dial and the music became softer, lower.

"Ever seen a gramophone this fine before?" he asked.

"No sir, she's a beauty." Actually, other than this one I'd never seen any gramophone before. I'd heard about them, and even seen a picture, but I'd never actually laid eyes on one.

"Got it in Boston. Top of the line. I'm goin' ta miss it."

"Miss it?" I asked, feeling confused.

"It will, of course, stay 'ere on the *Roosevelt*, and I'll be leaving with the rest of the expedition."

I guess that made sense, but somehow I didn't see him leaving the ship . . . that just seemed so un-Captain-like.

"Do ya know what's goin' ta be happenin' now?" he asked.

"I know we've finished unloadin' the ship."

"Should be done just after first light. Once everything is safely ashore, we're goin' to be movin' everything, overland to Cape Columbia, on the north coast."

"I thought we were on the north coast."

"Not north enough," Captain Bartlett explained. "Cape Columbia is about ninety miles northwest, and that's where we're going to be setting up base and wintering."

"I didn't know it would all 'appen right away."

"No choice. Today we have close to fourteen hours of daylight. By November seventh the sun will set and not rise until February." He paused. "That was what I wanted to talk to you about."

I waited for him to continue, not knowing what I had to do with any of these plans.

"Most of the crew, under the command of my first mate, will be stayin' aboard the *Roosevelt*. They'll be safeguardin' the ship."

"Safeguardin' it from what?" I asked.

"The ice. Could be nothing, but the ice could raft up, shift, could even scuttle the ship."

"Scuttle . . . you mean sink her?"

"It's a long winter and the ice is alive."

"And if she did sink?" I asked.

"The crew would winter on shore."

"An' then we'd 'ave to sledge home, right?" I asked.

"No choice." He paused. "But that's not somethin' we can predict or control. It's all in the hands of the Good Lord. I want to talk to you about somethin' you *can* control." Again he paused. "I always expected you'd be spending the winter aboard ship."

That was what I'd expected, too.

"But the Commander 'as said that he would like ta offer you the choice of comin' with the expedition, to Cape Columbia."

"And to the Pole?"

He laughed. "The run to the Pole is going to be just the Commander, myself, and a couple of the Eskimos. You would be comin' at least as far as the Cape and probably partway to the Pole, but not to the Pole itself. If you stay aboard ship you'll be warmer, better fed, and safer."

"Unless the ice sinks the ship."

"Not likely, but possible. You'll have time for your studies as a seaman under the tutelage of my first mate, and in your general schooling by other members of the crew. Mostly, though, you'll be playin' cards, sittin' around the stove in the mess with Cookie, and waitin' for us to return sometime late in April."

"An' if I come with you and the expedition?"

"I can only promise you that you'll work harder, eat less well, be cold most of the time and frozen some of it, and experience some things that will put your back to the wall and your soul and sanity in question." He paused again. "I think it would be better for a lad of your age to be stayin' aboard ship, but the Commander has asked that it be your choice. Well?"

I didn't answer right away. I didn't know what answer to give. I knew which choice was safer and easier. I just didn't know which was right.

"And just so you know, if you travel with us you'll still be studyin' and learnin'. The Eskimos, particularly Oatah, will school you in the ways of the north, in the ways of survival. Matthew has volunteered to work with me to school you in the more formal things . . . philosophy, Shakespeare, the Bible. Do not think that your lessons will be any less in the skin and snow and wood shelters ashore than they would be in the cabins of the ship. So?"

"Could I ask you a question, Cap'n?" I asked.

"Certainly."

"If it was you and not me . . . what would you do?"

He laughed. "I think ya know the answer to that question. You're not even fourteen and you're bein' offered the adventure of a lifetime."

"I'll pack my bag and be ready to leave at first light."

Chapter Twelve

November 25, 1908

I OPENED THE DOOR and was propelled in by a burst of wind and snow, causing me to tumble over! Before I'd even hit the floor of the shelter I was bombarded by voices yelling angrily about the cold that I was letting in! I scrambled to my feet and put my shoulder to the door. For a split second the wind seemed to be winning the battle and I dug in deeper, straining, struggling, finally winning and pushing the door closed.

I stamped my feet and brushed off my coat so I wouldn't trail snow across the room and get anybody any madder at me.

The room was lit by three oil lamps. As well there was a glow coming from the little stove that provided the feeble feelers of warmth that crept throughout the shelter. It was far from warm—you always needed to wear your coat and mukluks—but it was a tropical paradise compared to outside. I had no idea what the temperature was, but I knew that if you ventured out without your face and hands covered they'd be frostbitten in less than a minute.

The shelter was made out of those crates we'd been moving, with their lids facing inwards to make the walls—that explained why the men had been stacking them high.

I looked around the room. It certainly seemed smaller—but somehow safer—when we were all in here. Commander Peary was sitting at crates that he'd fashioned into a desk, writing in his journal. He was always writing in that journal, recording the events of the expedition "for posterity." That was a fancy way of saying for people to read about it.

Commander Peary had a real way with words. When he was talking, it sounded more like he was saying a speech, even if he was just saying ordinary things. More like something you'd read in a fancy play by Shakespeare or a Dickens story than somebody just talking over their back fence asking you about what you were having for dinner or what the weather was going to be tomorrow.

Mr. Marvin was sitting on the edge of his bed, reading. Dr. Goodsell was in his bed, under the covers, possibly asleep. Mr. MacMillan was writing a letter. He wrote a lot of letters. Considering that he wasn't going to be able to mail them until we returned to civilization—at least six months from now—it seemed like a curious thing to do with his time.

Over by the fire, sitting around a crate they were using as a table, were the Captain, George, and Matt. They were playing cards, but mostly that was just an excuse for them to sit and talk and debate and argue. I loved sitting just off to the side, listening to them. A whole lot of what they talked about made little sense to me. Discussions about philosophers I'd never read, places I hadn't visited, music I'd never heard, and words and ideas that were beyond me. Though, it did seem like I was understanding just a little bit more now than before.

I slumped into a seat beside the card players. I felt like I could relax now, knowing that the dogs were okay. It wasn't my job to watch the huskies, but I was pretty attached to a couple of the dogs, and I knew they liked me, too.

Usually the dogs were just staked down to the ice, but it was now too cold for even them to be out in the open. The Eskimos had built shelters out of snow and ice—they called them igloos—and the dogs were clustered together inside.

It was fascinating to watch those igloos being constructed. The Eskimos used long knives to carve out gigantic blocks of snow. The blocks were then piled up together in a little circle, getting smaller toward the top until a dome was formed. Little bits of snow were pushed into between the blocks—sort of like mortar between bricks—to block the wind and bind them together. Finally an opening was made. It was more like a tunnel than a door. It wasn't easy to get in—you had to practically lie down on your belly and crawl along.

It was almost warm inside those igloos. You were protected from the wind, and also the body heat of all the dogs together raised the temperature until it was only a few degrees below freezing. That was about as warm as the sledge dogs ever liked it.

George looked up from his cards. "So, Danny, how are the dogs?"

"I didn't check them all, but they seemed okay."

"Of course, they're fine!" Mr. Marvin called from across the room. "They're just dogs!"

"To the Eskimos they're more than dogs."

"I'm no Eskimo," Mr. Marvin sneered.

"Lucky Eskimos," George said under his breath, and Matt chuckled.

"Those dogs are important to the whole mission," the Captain said. "Without them there would be no possibility of reachin' the Pole. Good to check on them."

"Let the Eskimos take care of that sort of thing," Mr. Marvin barked.

"I think Danny is pretty attached to those dogs," George suggested.

Mr. Marvin scoffed. "Doesn't make sense to get attached to something you might have to eat!"

"Eat?" I asked in shock, turning to the Captain.

He shrugged his shoulders. "Sometimes dogs have to be eaten."

"We're going to eat the dogs?" I asked, not believing my ears.

"That's not the plan, but sometimes plans go awry," Captain Bartlett said. "Ya eat dogs or ya die."

"I'd rather die," I said.

"No you wouldn't," Matt said. "I've had to make that choice."

I gasped.

"Not a choice I ever wanted to make," he added.

"I have to agree with Matthew," Commander Peary said from across the room. He'd turned away from his makeshift desk. "I can say that of all the animals I've eaten, dog is one of the least appetizing."

"Tough, stringy," Matthew said.

"But in all fairness," Commander Peary said, "those dogs had been worked to within a whisker of death. Nothing left but sinew and string. Perhaps a fine, fat, pampered poodle might be a more tasty treat."

I shuddered, but the other men laughed. George's laugh cut through everybody else's. He loved to laugh.

"A poodle might be a welcome choice right about now," George said. "I'm certainly tired of seal and walrus, and I never want to taste another morsel of pemmican as long as I live!"

I agreed with that.

"You've eaten bear meat," Matt said. We'd all eaten polar bear. "Dog isn't very different from bear . . . it's got a more oily flavour but it's similar in texture."

I made a mental note to myself not to eat any more bear.

"I rather liked the bear meat," George said. "We've been out of bear for at least a week. I wonder when we might get more?"

"Just a matter of time," Matthew said, "until another bear wanders into camp."

"Only animal without the brains to avoid the hunter," Mr. Marvin said.

"Oh, it has brains," Captain Bartlett said. "It just hasn't had the experience to let it know that it should be afraid of us, or anything else. The polar bear is the most fierce killing machine God ever placed upon this planet."

"Most fierce?" George asked.

"No animal on earth is a match for a full-grown male of the species. Neither lion nor tiger can match it for muscle or mass or courage."

"I'd dare say an elephant would be more than its match," George said.

"An elephant is certainly larger, but it is, for the most part, a gentle soul. It does not eat or hunt humans . . . unlike the white bear. Do you know what a polar bear fears?"

Nobody said anything. Perhaps they were trying to come up with an answer.

"It fears nothing," the Captain said. "And do you know what it eats? . . . Everything."

That thought sent a shiver up my spine. There had been three polar bears killed within a dozen feet of this shelter, and more times than I could count bear tracks had been seen on the periphery of the camp.

"Perhaps a polar bear would eat anything, but I have my personal limits. I have to say that I will not be eating monkey again," Commander Peary said. "You ate monkey as well when we were in Nicaragua, didn't you, Matthew?"

He nodded his head. "I have had that, shall we say, pleasure. I would prefer dog to monkey."

"Understandable," Mr. Marvin said. "Eating a monkey must be like eating one of your cousins. It hasn't been that long since your people have been down from the trees themselves," he said, and laughed.

Nobody else laughed. I saw Matt's eyes flash with anger. Sometimes people said things—even Commander Peary—about Matthew being a Negro.

Even when they were said joking-like I knew Matt didn't like them.

"Not long since *any* of us have been down from the trees," George said. "At least, if you believe the works of Charles Darwin."

"Interesting book, that *Origin of Species*," Commander Peary said. "If Darwin is correct, we're all just a monkey's uncle."

"Or more correctly, a monkey's great-great-great-grandson," George said.

"Captain Bartlett," Commander Peary said, "you are a man of deep religious faith, one who is familiar with the Bible. I am curious to know what you make of this theory that man evolved from the lesser beasts."

"It's an interesting idea," the Captain said.

"But does it not conflict with the biblical account? God making heaven and earth in six days, and Adam being created from clay, moulded by the hands of God, and that all the other creatures were then created to be of service to man?"

"That is the word of the Bible," Captain Bartlett agreed. "But the Bible is only the words of man, not those of God himself."

"Some people would consider that a blasphemous statement," George said.

"And some people are damn fools," Captain Bartlett replied. "God spoke and people listened, but man is fallible. Besides, who's to say if God's day is the same as our day? Perhaps His six days are six thousand of our years? And who can say that He didn't craft creation through the means outlined by Darwin?" He paused. "What I do know is that, regardless of the creation, there is one animal that would be less appealing to eat than either monkey or dog or bear."

"Aahhh," Commander Peary said. "I think I would agree with that."

"As would all of us," George agreed. Matthew nodded his head as well.

I had no idea what animal they were referring to. I didn't want to eat a dog or monkey, but could they mean a pet cat, or perhaps something awful to the eye like an octopus or . . . ? Then I realized what they meant . . . at least, I thought I knew.

"Do you mean . . . ?" I let my sentence trail off. I couldn't bring myself to say the words.

"Cannibalism," Captain Bartlett said softly. "The eating of human beings."

"I've heard tell of people in Africa and the Pacific who eat people as part of their regular diets," George said.

"More like for festive occasions," Captain Bartlett said. "Or for ceremonies. Eatin' the heart and brain of your fallen enemy is said to give you his strength."

"I don't know about that," George said. "If he was so strong he wouldn't have lost and you wouldn't be eating him to begin with."

Again everybody laughed. I laughed too, but more out of nervousness.

"What is done by the primitives of the world is far different from what would be done by men of culture and breeding, civilized folks," Mr. Marvin said.

"Afraid that is not true, sir. Have you not heard of Sir John Franklin?" Captain Bartlett asked.

"Who has not?"

Slowly, reluctantly, I raised my hand. I didn't want people to know of my ignorance, but not as much as I wanted to not *be* ignorant.

"Franklin is thought by some to be the greatest polar explorer of all time," Captain Bartlett said, and then he turned to Commander Peary. "Present company excluded, of course."

Commander Peary nodded.

"Franklin was a Rear Admiral in the British Navy. He led expeditions through the Canadian Arctic in search of the North-West Passage to the Orient."

"Did he find it?" I asked.

"He made many discoveries, but ultimately all he found was death for himself and his entire crew," Captain Bartlett explained.

I didn't like the sound of that at all.

"And you believe there was cannibalism involved in that ill-fated ending?" George asked.

"There can be little doubt from the remains that were found. Knife marks on bones, the way the skeletal remains were scattered," Captain Bartlett said.

"Poor souls. To die in such a manner. Even partaking of human flesh did not preserve life but merely damned their souls," Mr. MacMillan said.

George shook his head slowly. "So sad, although I have a question." He paused. "Perhaps this question is a little bit indelicate."

"Too late for that," Captain Bartlett said. "Speak your mind."

"Well . . . if there is a noticeable difference between an old tough bull and a young heifer, then wouldn't there be a difference between an old dog and a young dog, perhaps?"

"I would imagine."

"How about between a boy and a man?"

Captain Bartlett looked at me. "So, you're wonderin' if perhaps Danny there would be more tender than Commander Peary or myself?"

"Well, yes," George said. He stood up, walked over, and lifted up one of my arms. "He's a little on the scrawny side, not a lot of meat, but he would be far more tender than an old sea-dog such as yourself."

This was a totally bizarre conversation. They were talking about what I would taste like if they had to eat me to survive!

"He might be more tender," Matt said, "but what if it's more like turkey?"

"You think he'd taste like turkey?" George asked.

"No, no. I imagine he'd taste more like *monkey*. I meant what if the variety of the meat was like turkey. Some people like light meat and some like dark. Would I be dark meat?"

Commander Peary walked over to join the men at the card table. He put a hand on Matt's shoulder. "This talk has been most interesting, but there is much to be done tomorrow. Perhaps it is now time for us all to turn in for the night."

George stepped up onto the crate. "'Good night, good night! Parting is such sweet sorrow that I shall say good night till it be morrow!'"

"You don't look like no Juliet," I said.

"Bravo, Danny!" George said, clapping his hands.

I broke into a smile. "Everybody knows *Romeo and Juliet*," I mumbled.

"Not everybody," Matthew said.

"Obviously you have been taking your studies seriously," Captain Bartlett said.

In the quiet times in the evenings both Matt and the Captain talked to me about things, or read to me, or had me read. Some of what they talked about went way over my head, or bored me to tears, but other stuff was truly amazing. I think I loved best when they just talked to me—or discussed something between them. The best discussions were when they didn't agree and they debated and argued. Even when I didn't understand everything they said, it was all pretty amazing.

"Now it's my turn for a quote. 'Sorrow breaks seasons and reposing hours, makes the night morning and the noontide night.'"

"I'd hazard a guess and say it's Shakespeare," George said with a laugh.

"Would anybody care to be more specific?" Captain Bartlett asked.

There was no answer.

"Matthew?" the Captain asked.

Matt smiled. "*Richard the Third* . . . act one, scene four, spoken by Brakenbury."

Captain Bartlett touched his hand to the side of his head and offered a salute. I wasn't surprised by Matt knowing the answer. The two of them—he and Captain Bartlett—were always trading quotes . . . Shakespeare, Dickens, the Bible. Matt was more than just my tutor, he was my example of what somebody could do, how much they could learn, without ever having gone very far in school.

"'Oh weary night, oh long and tedious night . . . '" Matt said.

Captain Bartlett stood up and walked over to one of the lamps, extinguishing it, and the room became even dimmer.

"George, would you care to field this one and show the benefits of a higher education at Cornell?" Captain Bartlett asked.

"I would love that opportunity. Unfortunately, I have the opportunity but not the knowledge."

"Anybody else care to venture a guess?"

"A Midsummer Night's Dream?" I asked.

"Correct!" Captain Bartlett exclaimed. George slapped me on the back and Commander Peary looked pleased— although not as pleased as Matt.

"I believe it is Helena speaking, act three . . . perhaps scene two or three," Captain Bartlett said.

"Scene two," Matt replied.

Captain Bartlett extinguished a second lamp, leaving just one burning. I moved toward my bed while there was still light.

"Let me leave you with one final quote. 'O grim-looked night, O night with hue so black . . . '"

As he said the final word he extinguished the last lamp and the room was thrown into darkness. It took a few seconds for my eyes to adjust—it wasn't total darkness because there was still some light coming from the stove. I could just make out the shadowy figures of the men settling into their beds.

"Well?" Captain Bartlett's voice asked from the darkness.

"Act five, scene one, *A Midsummer Night's Dream*," Matt replied.

"Correct. And at this point a midsummer's night is nothing more than a dream. Good night, gentlemen."

Chapter Thirteen

December 3, 1908

THE WIND WAS RAGING outside the walls of our little shelter. It was so strong that even the canvas roof was rippling. The sound of the wind was a constant. It didn't always make the same sound, but it was always there in the background. Sometimes it was faint, other times a whistle or a dull rumble. Sometimes it roared like a wild animal or the passing of a train. Stranger, sometimes it sounded like a human voice crying out, or laughing, or even speaking. In the middle of the night, lying in the dark, if I listened hard enough I could almost make out the words it was saying. There was a rhythm, like a poem, like it was saying the same word over and over, or maybe a whole phrase. There were times when I thought if I just listened harder, concentrated every fibre of my being, I could understand. But I never could. Maybe it's not that I wasn't listening hard enough, but that the wind was speaking a different language. Inuktitut. That would make sense. The Arctic wind *would* speak Inuktitut, the language of the people of the north.

Along with the wind there was one other sound that was almost always there at night. Snoring. Both

Commander Peary and the Captain snored almost every night. Dr. Goodsell did some nights, too, and occasionally George and Mr. Marvin added to the chorus. And, just like the wind, the snoring came in different sounds and textures, from whistles, to snorts, to rumbles, to roars.

It would start with a snore from one corner, and then, like an answer, a second snore would pipe up from the far side of the shelter. It sounded like they were talking back and forth. Other times the sound just kept growing as each successive snore was added on top of the other until it made a strange symphony. Certainly nothing that Bach or Mozart would have taken credit for. At those times it would be loud—loud enough to keep me awake.

The noise was disturbing, but it was also reassuring. I knew that outside the walls of our shelter there was nothing but snow and ice and bone-chilling cold for thousands of miles. But here I was surrounded by the members of the expedition. Maybe I couldn't see them in the dark, but I could hear them, and I knew they were there to protect and care for me. I could lie in bed and let the wind and the snoring—just another form of wind—sing me to sleep.

But that night I heard a different sound. It was more like a cry . . . no, a whine . . . no, something else, something I'd never heard before. Then it was gone . . . if it had ever been real to begin with. It had sounded almost like an animal crying out in pain.

It came again. I perked up my ears a little trying to hear. It had definitely come from outside . . . and was that the dogs barking and baying? Maybe. But it didn't matter. If the dogs were making a racket somebody else would hear it and do something about it. Unless everybody else thought the same thing . . .

I pulled the blanket down and was hit by a wave of cold. I threw my legs over the edge and reached around for my mukluks in the dark. I found one and tried to slide my foot inside. The leather was cold and stiff and I had to force it in. I did the same with the second. I was already wearing my parka but it was unbuttoned and I fumbled with the buttons, fastening them.

I stood up and, with one hand on my bunk for balance and guidance, I started toward the door. I had to check out the sound. Probably nothing except a couple of the dogs fighting. Probably. But I had to check.

Part of me wanted to wake somebody up, to tell them what I was doing, or even ask them to come along. George would have come along if I'd asked him, I was sure. But I wasn't going to ask. No sense in waking somebody up for nothing. Probably there was no sense in me even going out to check. But I was going to go anyway.

I worked my way to the door. I put my hand on the knob and readied myself. If I wasn't careful, when I released the latch the door would blow wide open, and the cold air and snow rushing in would wake somebody or everybody else in the shelter. I put my shoulder against the door to stop that from happening. I slowly eased it open. It didn't push back. I could still hear the wind, but it must have been coming from a different direction.

I could hear the dogs barking more clearly now. They always barked a lot, but there was something different this time. I went to step outside but stopped myself. First I reached over and took one of the rifles that was leaning against the wall. The metal of the barrel felt freezing against my skin. I hadn't put gloves on. Maybe I should go back to my bunk and get them or—the dogs were barking louder, almost frantically.

I stepped outside and pulled the door closed behind me. It was dark—it was always dark—but it was brighter than inside. The moon was big and bright and gave off enough light to allow me to clearly see the shelter across from us. I circled around the side of the shelter to where the dogs were kept and—I stopped dead in my tracks. There was a polar bear—a gigantic polar bear—standing beside one of the igloos!

I quickly retreated to the safety of the shelter and peeked around the corner.

The dogs—inside the igloo and unseen—could sense the bear . . . smell the bear. So that was why they were barking so wildly. The bear knew about the dogs as well. It circled around the base of the igloo, sniffing, prodding it with one of its front paws. It knew there was something inside—something to eat—but it didn't seem to know how to get the food out, or how to get in.

Suddenly the bear reared up on its back legs. It raised a paw high above its head and then smashed it against the side of the igloo! The igloo exploded, ice blocks went flying into the air, and the whole side collapsed. Instantly half a dozen dogs came charging out of the opening. The bear swung its paw again and one of the dogs went flying! It landed ten feet away, crashing against the ice with a terrible thud and rolling. When it tried to get back to its feet, it stumbled, staggered, and then collapsed. Its blood was staining the ice!

The other dogs scrambled around the bear, snapping at its heels and barking hysterically. The bear, standing on its back legs, towered above the dogs and swung its front right paw, trying to hit them. They danced around, in and out, snapping and snarling, somehow managing to avoid the bear's deadly attempts to— It hit a second dog and knocked it through the air! The dog skidded to a stop, got back to its feet, and scrambled to rejoin the attack. More dogs streamed out of the gash in the side of the igloo. There were now at least a dozen dogs attacking the bear. Their attempts were almost useless, though—the bear was so much bigger and protected by thick fur and rolls of fat.

I couldn't just stand there and watch. I stepped out from behind the shelter—I needed to be in the open to fire. I was terrified the bear would see me, but it was too occupied with the dogs to even notice. I brought the gun up to my eye and looked through the sights, right at the bear's chest. It was so big and I was so close I couldn't miss, but would I kill it or just injure it? Once it was shot it *would* notice me, and nothing's more dangerous than a wounded bear. I raised my sights higher. I wanted to put a shot into its head. I tried to draw a bead, but as the bear engaged in its deadly dance with the dogs it jumped and jived and scrambled so much that I couldn't be sure of a shot. I might miss, or even hit one of the dogs by mistake.

The bear reared up onto its back legs again and suddenly I had a clean shot. I levelled the rifle, pulled back the bolt, and fired. The rifle recoiled against my shoulder, sending me reeling backwards! A split second later the bear jumped and roared in pain as the bullet buried itself in its neck and a flash of blood exploded outward! Almost in slow motion the bear turned around, looking for the source of its pain. It moved its head from side to side, swinging it back and forth, searching. Finally it stopped moving and stared directly at me, blood still gushing out and staining its fur. It dropped to all fours and charged me!

I fumbled with the rifle, fumbled with the bolt, trying to draw a second bullet into the chamber as the bear rushed toward me, bigger and bigger. And then—it swooshed right by me! I spun around and watched as the bear raced away, the dogs trailing after it, snapping at its heels. The bear staggered and then fell to the ice, skidding to a stop. The dogs set to it, snapping and biting. I expected it to get back up, turn, swing, fight, but it didn't. It just lay there on the ice. Dead. It was dead! The dogs ripped at its skin, tearing off patches of fur.

All at once there were people all around: Eskimos and members of the expedition—the Captain, George, Matt— people streaming out of the shelters, all trying to make sense of the sounds that had roused them . . . the dogs, the scream of the bear, the gunshot. I stood there frozen in place as they swirled and swarmed around me.

Captain Bartlett got to me first. "Danny?"

I motioned with the end of the rifle toward the bear, lying there, the dogs still attacking its lifeless form. I walked toward the bear. There was a trail of blood stain-ing the snow. The dogs were all over it—six or seven of them—snarling, climbing on top of it, biting its leg, ripping off pieces of fur and flesh. A couple of the Eskimos started to grab the dogs, pulling them away. They didn't want to leave and fought hard, snapping at their handlers. The dogs were in a blood lust, standing over their fallen enemy. Finally the last dog was forcibly removed and dragged away.

I stood over top of the bear. Absently, gently, I nudged it with my foot as if I were trying to wake it from its sleep. It didn't wake. It didn't move. It didn't even budge. I bent down. It just lay there on the ice, its head and neck at an awkward angle, its whole side covered with blood. Its tongue was hanging out of the side of its mouth and its eyes were open, reflecting the moonlight.

"One shot?" George asked.

I nodded.

"Pretty good shooting."

I nodded again.

"Danny, get back inside," Captain Bartlett said. "You're shaking . . . badly."

"He doesn't have gloves or a hat, no wonder," George said.

I was shaking but it wasn't from the cold. My legs suddenly felt weak and my knees started to buckle.

George grabbed one arm and Matt the other. I didn't resist as they led me back to the shelter.

Chapter Fourteen

December 25, 1908

"FOR THINE IS THE KINGDOM, the power and the glory, forever and ever, Amen," Captain Bartlett said.

"Amen," we all answered in unison.

I lifted my head.

"It is said that God is everywhere. Look about," Captain Bartlett said.

We were standing on the ice. The camp was on the shore, in the distance, lit by the moon and the millions and millions of stars that twinkled overhead. There was no sound . . . no wind. It was as though even the wind had stopped to listen to the Captain's sermon, to praise and honour the birth of Jesus. A few months ago I would have believed that was a ridiculous thought, but now, I wasn't so sure. Why couldn't the wind have a spirit, the ice, the sky? The Eskimo stories that talked about such things made just as much sense to me as those in the Bible.

I looked down at the little manger that Captain Bartlett had fashioned out of one of the discarded crates. Inside was a baby Jesus doll made of sealskin and cloth. One of the women had made it. It was beautifully crafted and looked so lifelike that I almost thought it might open its eyes, smile, and be real. It had hair as dark as night, olive-coloured skin, and although the eyes were closed, I imagined beneath those closed lids they were dark, Eskimo eyes.

Oh sure, there was a bit of a grumbling from a couple of members of the expedition who thought it wasn't proper for Jesus to look like an Eskimo, but I thought, why not? Maybe it wasn't blond-haired and blue-eyed like the Jesus in the church books back home, but Captain Bartlett said the people of Bethlehem were all dark-skinned, dark-eyed Arabs who looked more like the Eskimos than any of us.

I didn't know about any of that, but I knew my Bible well enough to know that God made man in His image, and we were all God's children . . . each and every one of us. I wasn't sure about that Darwin guy and the whole theory of evolution—no way I was related to apes or monkeys—but even if Darwin was right, it still meant we were all related, all brothers and sisters and cousins—all family.

I looked down at the little manger. I wondered what Jesus would make of any of this. Standing on the ice in the freezing Arctic temperatures, the sun nowhere to be seen even though it was nearly noon, all of us dressed in layers of clothing, I couldn't imagine any scene farther away from Bethlehem.

Every member of the party—crew, expedition, and Eskimo—stood there listening to the Captain. The Eskimos were mostly not Christian, and only a few had a good grasp of English, but they had all come to the service. They were like that. Curious, and polite, but mostly respectful. Maybe they didn't understand the words, or would agree with what they meant if they did, but they were prepared to listen. They all bowed their heads when we did, yelled out "Amen" when the Captain did, and nodded their heads enthusiastically, following our lead.

Being around the Captain and Matt, I'd certainly learned a lot about the Bible. They could both quote verses for almost any occasion. There was a lot of learning in that Good Book.

I'd also learned about Eskimo beliefs, their religion. It was all told in stories, none of it written down, just passed on from person to person, father to son and mother to daughter, from one generation to another. There were times I'd go and sit in the shelter with the Eskimos. It was awfully crowded, but they always made room for me. I'd sit down, join them in a circle, and listen to their stories. They loved to tell stories. Of course I understood less Inuktitut than most of them understood English, but still I listened. Oatah would translate some of it—give me the meaning of the story—but what I really loved was just listening to the voices rising up or getting all quiet, watching the gestures, or acting—pretending to run or throw a spear or whatever—and the way everybody reacted. People would cheer or hiss or clap or whistle in response.

Even more interesting than the stories was the way I was treated. Everybody, but especially the women, was really kind to me. They were always talking to me—using what little bits of broken English they knew—and patting me on the back, bringing me food to eat. I remember the first time I was offered a piece of raw blubber to eat. I wanted to spit it out, but I didn't. I chewed it slowly, almost gagging before I swallowed it down. Now, it still wasn't my favourite food—I think all meat should be cooked—but I could eat it. Certainly it wasn't any worse than eating pemmican.

At first I thought they were all being nice to me because I was white and different. Then I noticed how they treated all the children in the party. Eskimos love children. Not just their own, but any child. They were just so kind and caring, and they made me feel like I was almost part of their family. That would have been something, to be part of a family that big. If you lost your mother or father there'd still be others around to step up and take care of you.

Captain Bartlett came into the Eskimo shelter sometimes, but the only other person who visited there regularly was Matt. Of course he knew their language, but it was more than that. He cared for them, showed respect, knew their customs. Some of them called him *maktak kabloona,* meaning black white man, but he was as much Eskimo as he was black or white . . . he was a combination of all of those things. They also called Matt one other thing, *Miy Paluk*. It meant "Dear Matt," and that was how he was treated.

"As we stand here, thousands of years and thousands of miles removed from the birth of Jesus, I ask you to look up," Captain Bartlett said as he raised his eyes skyward, and we all followed his gaze to the heavens above us.

"The millions of stars that form the ceiling above our 'eads are the same stars seen by Joseph and Mary. Perhaps the North Star," he said, pointing directly at it, "was the one followed by the Three Wise Men as they travelled to pay homage to the baby Jesus." He paused as we all looked at it. "As we stand 'ere beneath that same star, we are small, an' alone, and fragile." He paused. "But remember, it is not just the star that looks down upon us. We are under the loving gaze of the Lord. He is strong and powerful, and we are never alone because He is with us. We are His children—all of us are His children—and God will care for us. Let us go forth, our souls bathed in the warmth of that love. Let us now bow our 'eads in prayer."

I bowed my head as Captain Bartlett started to pray. I listened to the first part, and then my mind drifted away. I wasn't thinking about Jesus as much as I was about what was going to happen tomorrow . . . the race . . . the big dog-sledge race.

Chapter Fifteen

December 26, 1908

I BENT DOWN beside my lead dog—the name I'd given him was Lightning, because he had a white zigzag bolt across his chest. I scratched him behind the ear, right where he loved being rubbed, and he pressed his head against my hand. He and Blackie were my favourite dogs, but Blackie was a little guy, not strong enough to be a lead. Lightning was big and strong. Not the biggest or the strongest, but a lead dog had to have more than just strength. It had to listen to what it was told and get that message to the rest of the team. Sometimes that meant snarling or growling or nipping at the other dogs, but mostly it just involved pulling them in the right direction.

I looked down the line at the rest of my team. Ten dogs, including Blackie, all hand-picked, all the dogs I wanted. I knew each and every one of the huskies, what they were like, and that was no small task. We'd started out at camp with close to two hundred dogs and we'd lost twenty-three. Two were killed by the polar bear and the others had died of sickness.

I remembered when I couldn't even tell the dogs apart by looking at them. Sure, some were bigger and some smaller, male and female, and their coats were somewhat different in colour and pattern, but a whole lot of them looked pretty much the same. At first I'd learned by necessity. When I was cleaning up after them on the ship I had to learn which ones to avoid if I didn't want to get bitten. Then, as I got to know the dogs, I just grew to like them—at least some of them. Oatah had helped me to understand the dogs, what to look for. He'd explained to me that what made a good sledge dog didn't necessarily make for a good companion dog, and vice-versa. Now, I had a good team hooked up to my komatik.

I guess I liked being around the dogs because they reminded me of the dog I used to own. Candy was her name. She was a great dog, but we had to get rid of her when my mother died. My sister had room for me in her home, but not for Candy. Funny, I think I cried more about having to give Candy away than I did about my mother dying. After all, losing Candy was a bolt out of the blue. With my mother, I'd seen it coming—knew how sick she was—and there really wasn't anybody to blame. It was just God's will . . . I guess for a while that was who I was mad at. Probably it was not smart to be mad at God, 'cause what if He decided to get mad back? Especially up here, in a place where so much could happen so suddenly.

Candy was born two doors down from our house, and my mother brought me to the Hendersons' place to look at the new litter of puppies. I think she was trying to take my mind off the fact that my father's ship was late returning. I wasn't worried, but I knew she was. Candy was just a little scrap of black-and-white fur, even smaller than the other tiny puppies. She was the runt of the litter, and

Mrs. Henderson told my mother—in a voice she thought I couldn't hear—that the little one "would be dead before the morn." Mrs. Henderson was old and half deaf and her quiet voice was pretty loud.

When we got home I asked my mother if I could have the little pup. She told me yes . . . if it lived. I was little but I wasn't stupid. I figured she'd only said that because she thought it was going to die. But it didn't die. That little puppy kept fighting, kept growing, and survived. My mother said it was a lot like me.

I was a little runt too, born too early and too small, and nobody thought I was going to live. I spent my first days in a little box, all bundled up, right by the stove, the heat of the fire pulsing life into my body. I was supposed to die, but I didn't. I lived, and so did Candy. We were bonded together at birth, even though those births were seven years apart.

And my mother kept her word. I guess she didn't have the heart to say no after we got the news that my father's ship had gone down and there were no survivors. The puppy was my present. Not a birthday present. A death-day present. Candy was born the day my father's ship was supposed to return—the day, we later learned, that it was lost. My father's death brought that dog into my life. My mother's death took Candy away.

Funny, when the men were talking about not getting too attached to something you might have to eat, I was thinking how it was wise not to get too attached to *anything* you might lose, and that meant *everything*.

Understanding the dogs meant seeing beneath what they *looked* like to what they *were* like. Every one was different. It was easy enough to see which huskies were the biggest, but that wasn't enough to know if they would be good sledge dogs. You had to know what they were like. Just as important, you had to know how they acted when they were around different dogs. Some dogs just plain didn't like each other and fought. Others liked each other too much and didn't listen. Especially didn't listen to English. I'd learned enough Inuktitut to give the basic orders, but I wished I knew more.

Oatah told me that the most important thing about the dogs was maybe the hardest to know. It wasn't the size of the dog that mattered, but the size of the spirit within the dog that counted. Some dogs had a spirit that wouldn't allow them to stop or lose.

It seemed to me that everything Oatah taught me about dogs didn't apply only to the dogs, it applied to people as well. You had to look for the spirit, the heart, not the size of the person carrying it around. Being small meant nothing if your spirit was large.

The dog-sledge race was Captain Bartlett's idea. He wanted the members of the expedition to become more skilled sledge-men, and he thought a little competition would bring out the best in everybody. And he was right. Everybody started taking all this race stuff pretty seriously. Nobody wanted to lose. I think he asked me to be part of it only so that everybody would dig a little bit deeper, 'cause nobody wanted to lose to a fourteen-year-old boy. They saw the boy, but they didn't know about the spirit inside. I knew that because of the way they had chosen their dogs—get the biggest, pick by weight and height but not by spirit.

George was the most excited about the race. The athlete in him loved to compete, and he'd be hard to beat. He'd chosen a good team, but he was also the strongest, fastest person in the competition. He'd be able to run alongside the sledge longer than the rest of us, and that meant his dogs wouldn't tire as quickly.

Above all, everyone wanted to prove to Commander Peary that he'd made a good choice in bringing them along on this expedition. And then maybe, just maybe, if they showed him they were good enough, he would take them all the way to the Pole.

Stretched along the start line were the seven teams in the race—the four members of the expedition, two crew members, Alex and Sandy, and me. Standing, sitting on snowbanks, talking, and laughing, every single member of the party was there. I was nervous enough about having to race, but it made it worse to have everybody watching. I didn't expect to win, but I was afraid of embarrassing myself in front of the whole world, and that's what it felt like. Maybe it was only sixty people or so, but that was everybody in the world I was living in. The rest of the world, my sister and her family, heck, all the people in Newfoundland and even New York, didn't exist any more. As far as I knew, everybody who existed in the entire world was right here, watching.

"You ready, Danny?" Matt asked.

"I'm a little nervous."

"A little nervous is good."

He walked down the line of dogs, patting one, pulling the harness of another. I knew he was checking up to see if I'd tied the leads right. I might have been offended, but I knew it was being done for the right reason.

"Have you memorized the course?" he asked.

"What's to memorize? I'm just gonna be followin' George."

"That will work if he doesn't get too far ahead of you, or if you're not in front of him."

"I don't think we have to worry too much about me bein' in the lead," I said. I was worried about being left behind, though. "Don't I just follow the markers?"

"The markers are there. Alternating blue and red."

Matt and the Captain had marked the race course, using the usual pemmican cans. Of course I'd still have to keep my eyes open. They'd be spaced out pretty far because it was a ten-mile course, curving in a big circle right back to the starting line.

"I stay to the left of the blue and the right of the red, right?" I asked, not feeling one hundred percent sure.

"That's correct. Just remember: red is right. Alliteration."

"Alliter . . . ?"

"It means they start with the same letter. It makes it easy to remember."

"Oh, okay, sure, I can remember that. Hey Matt, can I ask you a question?"

"Of course."

"If this is just a race, why did they load all this stuff on our sledges? Wouldn't we go faster if there was no weight?"

"Definitely, but this is to help people get accustomed to driving a loaded komatik. Besides, the load includes things you might need."

"How could I need all of this in ten miles?" I asked, pointing to the bulge on the sledge. Everything was tied down and hidden beneath a sheet of canvas.

"Hopefully you won't need any of it. But you might." He reached down and pulled out a rifle. "I know you know how to use this."

I nodded my head. I also knew what I might have to use it for. There had been polar bear tracks by the camp just yesterday.

"There are also dry clothes in case you go through the ice and—"

"But the ice is solid, completely solid, isn't it?"

"Most places almost three feet thick. But just in case."

"Then shouldn't the dogs be hooked up differently?" I asked. They were all in a straight line, not fanned out.

"No need for that. You get better speed this way, and there's almost no chance that you'll be going through."

"Almost no chance, but *some* chance," I said.

"Tiny."

"So I ask ya again, if it's a tiny chance, why bring along the extra clothes?" I asked.

"Even if it's only a one-in-a-thousand chance, aren't those extra few pounds of clothes worth it to save your life?"

That was hard to argue with. "But that can't all be clothes," I said pointing to the mound under the canvas.

"There's a sealskin tent, a little stove, some sleeping skins, and enough food for three days for you and the dogs."

I was shocked. "But this is only going to take four or five hours, isn't it?"

"More like seven or eight, and that's if you run fast and clean. Running clean isn't the problem. If a blizzard blows in, there's no telling. It could be three or four days."

I almost felt sick to my stomach. "Do you think that could happen?"

"The weather looks good," Matt said. "No clouds on the horizon."

That made me feel better.

"But storms can come across the ice pretty fast. If that happens, you just make camp and wait it out."

"By myself?"

"Maybe a few of you might be together. Just don't panic. Remember that the Captain and I are going to be driving sledges along the route as well."

"You're part of the race?"

He laughed. "Wouldn't be a race if I was part of it. We're going to leave a few hours later, just to make sure everybody is moving. If you break down or have to camp, you know we'll come and find you. Just stay on the course."

"Don't worry, I'm not plannin' on takin' any side trips."

"That's safe, but not necessarily smart," Matt said.

"And how would goin' off the course be smart?" I asked, feeling confused.

Matt didn't answer right away. Instead he moved very close and started to speak in a low voice, like he was afraid of being overheard. "If you don't go off course you won't be able to win."

"Matt, I wasn't even thinkin' about winnin'."

"You *should* think about winning," he said.

"You think I can win?" I asked, incredulous.

"No, I don't think there's any way you can beat George . . . that is, unless you go *off course*."

Now I was just plain confused.

"Let me ask you a question. Do you want to be sitting here at the camp waving when the expedition finally leaves for the Pole?"

"I don't think I have much choice in that."

"There's only one way you'll have any choice. But it doesn't matter unless you want to come along. Do you want to come along?"

I had to think. It would have been easier if I had made the decision to stay with the ship in the first place. I would have been saved hours of back-breaking work. I would have been warm and safe. But I was glad I'd come. If I left here for the Pole, across the frozen but unfreezing ice, I'd be exposed to open water, more cold, more danger. I knew what I wanted to do.

"I'd like to be part of it . . . but can I?"

"It depends. The Commander will take the best sledge drivers he has. You need to show him you can drive a sledge and handle the dogs."

Now I understood. "I need to win the race."

"Not necessarily win, but do well, show him something."

"And if I do well, I can go to the Pole?"

He laughed. "The only person who's definitely going to the Pole is the Commander. He's also promised Captain Bob. Me, I have a good shot. You're a long shot, but you have to remember that the Commander owes you a debt for saving the life of his daughter. If you can give him reason to believe you should be coming along, who knows?"

"So . . . what do I have to do if I want to win the race?" I asked.

"Well . . . there's this one spot . . . "

Chapter Sixteen

I STOOD THERE thinking about what Matt had told me to do. I could do it. I was positive. I just didn't know if either I *should* or I *would*. After all, taking a shortcut was cheating . . . wasn't it?

All I had to do was keep track of the markers. At the tenth blue marker the course was going to shoot off sharply to the right to get around a large pressure ridge. Pressure ridges are places where the ocean currents push the ice up into the air, sometimes ten or even twenty feet high. Matt said that the ridge ran for almost two miles and then the course cut back to the left again. If I could climb over the ridge I'd gain almost two miles of running on everybody else. He said I'd have to do some chopping and maybe even unload the komatik but I could do that a lot faster than they could do the two miles. As well, my dogs would be two miles less tired than the other teams.

Matt said it wasn't unfair. He said I shouldn't think of it as cheating. What I'd be doing was taking a risk. Maybe it would turn out to be a shortcut, but maybe I'd just be making things harder for myself if I got hung up on the ice. It was a gamble, and I could only hope that it would get me to the finish line faster!

I was nervous. Despite the cold I could feel the palms of my hands sweating. I'd been on the ice before for short trips, but this was different. I'd be on the ice for a long time, going off course, and out of sight of other people, by myself.

Oatah came up, along with three Eskimo women—one was his wife. All four had big smiles. His wife pulled something out of the inside of her parka. It was the baby Jesus!

"Here," Oatah said, gesturing to the doll that she was now holding out to me.

I took it from her hands. "Why is she givin' it to me?"

"Komatik."

"What about my sledge?"

Oatah said something to the woman and she answered. He nodded his head and then turned back to me.

"Baby Jesus needs ride."

The three women smiled and giggled. Oatah's wife took the doll from me, pulled out a piece of rawhide, and tied it firmly in place on the top of my load. I looked at the little doll. It looked peaceful, eyes closed, sound asleep. Turned out I wouldn't be alone out there after all. I had baby Jesus with me!

There was a lot of barking going on up and down the line. The dogs knew that they were going out on the ice and they were excited. They didn't necessarily like pulling a heavy load but they did like running and being out in the open.

"Drivers, please go to your teams!" Captain Bartlett called out.

I gave baby Jesus a little pat and then walked alongside of my huskies. As I passed each dog I grabbed the harness and gave it a strong tug to make sure they were all tied in securely. Better safe than sorry. No snags, no loose leads. My team was ready.

"Drivers take your marks!" Captain Bartlett yelled.

I hurried behind the sledge and grabbed the lead in my hand. I knew I had to get off quickly. The course was wide here, but when we hit the shoreline the path both narrowed and dipped. If you got behind at the beginning it would be hard to make up that time.

"Ready!" Captain Bartlett yelled. He held a pistol in his right hand and had it aimed straight up into the sky.

Bang!

I started, jumping slightly, and the sledge surged forward before I could even yell for the dogs to go—they knew what was happening. I held onto the handles and the lead but I didn't jump onto the back, not even one foot. I ran behind, almost pushing the sledge forward instead of adding extra weight for the dogs. We had to get ahead of as many of the others as we could before the narrows.

I tried to focus only on my team but I could sense and see out of the corner of my eye the other teams. I was pulling away from the team to my right. I was even with his lead dog, which put me a full sledge ahead. To the left, beside me, was George. His team was slightly ahead, but not much. If I could keep George in my sights then nobody else would be able to touch me—he was that much stronger and faster. I looked past him and toward the other sledges to the left. They were even farther back. I was in second place!

George let out a whoop that even overpowered the barking of the dogs. It was a cry of sheer delight. Almost instinctively, before I could even think of it, I screamed out a reply. But why not? This was amazing!

I put one foot up onto the runner and then jumped on with the second. George was in front of me, in the lead. He was still running instead of riding. Was he gonna run the whole way? He was opening up a big lead already. He had to be twenty yards ahead. There was no way he could be caught. If I'd been Commander Peary, I knew who I'd take with me to the Pole.

I looked over my shoulder. I was happy with what I saw. The other teams had fallen into a line. The closest sledge to me was at least five lengths distant. It was Mr. Marvin's. Sometimes he wasn't the friendliest person on the expedition, but I had to hand it to him, he knew how to handle a team. He also knew a lot about the Arctic. Behind him, the other four sledges were trailing by different distances. I couldn't tell who was who because of the similarity of the parkas. If things worked out, I wouldn't need to know because they'd just get farther and farther behind and—

"Aaaahhh!" I screamed as the sledge dipped down and I was thrown off the runners. I held onto the handles. I was being dragged along as we dipped off the shore and onto the ocean ice. I struggled to pull myself up, get to my feet. My body bounced and I was badly jarred by the bumps and scrapes! I wanted to let go, I wanted to yell out in pain! Instead I worked harder and pulled myself up and put a knee down on one of the runners. I held on, got the second knee on, and then hauled myself back up to a standing position.

I felt a gust of cold air against my chest—there was a rip in my parka! It wasn't big, but it was gonna chill me pretty fast. Still holding on with one hand, I took off my mitt and started to stuff it into the hole. It was a tight fit, but it worked. I reached down into my pocket and grabbed another mitt—I'd stashed a spare pair. Your hands got sweaty and damp and a new dry pair was good to have. At least I still had one extra mitt.

I jumped off the komatik, still holding on to the handle with one hand. I started running and I felt a sore spot on my left leg—I'd probably smashed it against something when I was being dragged. It didn't feel good, but it didn't feel bad enough to stop me.

Up ahead George had opened up his lead even more. It looked as though he was still running. As I watched, he passed between the first pair of markers, blue to his left and red to his right. I had to keep count, and I had to be certain. If I went off course at the wrong place, I wouldn't finish the race at all.

George was up ahead, going fast, still pulling away slightly, but still within my sight. That was good. All I had to do was follow his route. Hopefully he was finding the best path around the ridges.

Anybody who had never been up north on the ocean ice would figure that the frozen sea was just smooth ice. It was nothing like that. Aside from the drifts there were the pressure ridges—some small, almost like little ripples on the surface, but others as high as a house. They were forming all the time. Maybe the surface of the ocean was frozen, but just below the ice the water was alive and constantly moving. The ice was solid and strong, but the currents were much, much stronger.

More dangerous than the ice rising up into pressure ridges was it opening up underneath your feet. There was less worry about that now because of the extreme cold, but it was still on every driver's mind.

I heard barking behind me. I jumped onto the runners and looked back over my shoulder. It was Mr. Marvin. His team was getting closer. The dogs were barking excitedly. He was running beside the sledge, screaming out commands. He was strong and determined and pretty good with a team. I hadn't expected to keep ahead of him for very long anyway, but I wasn't ready to give up just yet.

I held the lead and jumped down off the runners. I ran behind the sledge, yelling out encouragement to my dogs. They began barking more enthusiastically and picked up their pace. They could hear the other team behind us, and I think they just knew it was a race and they didn't want to be beaten. They dug in deeper.

Off to the left we passed by another blue marker. I cut close, trying to follow the route I'd watched George travel. I was moving so fast that I was gaining on him. He was still far, far ahead, but I was closing the gap. Almost on cue he cut to the right and vanished behind a large pressure ridge. I had a rush of uneasiness, not seeing George, not having him in my sight.

I could still hear Mr. Marvin's dogs pursuing me, but now that seemed less threatening and more reassuring. I couldn't see George, but Mr. Marvin still had me in his sights. He wasn't always the nicest man but he was smart and knew what he was doing. If I got into any trouble he'd be there.

I noticed that the barking didn't seem to be coming from the back now as much as from the side. I jumped back onto the runners so I could turn around and have a look. Mr. Marvin was still behind me but he had taken a different tack and was well off to the left-hand side. Maybe he'd seen a better route, one that George had missed. Either I had to move faster to stay ahead—if he had found a shorter way—or this was my chance to put some distance between us if he had made a bad choice. I couldn't be sure, but it looked as though he was going to try to find a way to the far left of the pressure ridge. I jumped back down and started to run along.

As I ran I kept turning to the side, trying to keep an eye on Mr. Marvin's progress. It was hard to tell if he was gaining or falling behind, but I did know that the distance between us was growing as he angled off to the side. Was he taking a better line than the one I was following—the one George had taken? I couldn't think about that. I trusted George, and I'd made my decision. No matter what, this was the way I was going.

Mr. Marvin was still running along beside his team, moving hard. I was almost at the pressure ridge where George had made his right turn and vanished from sight. I'd be there in a few seconds and then the race between us would be going on out of sight. I looked back one more time before I took the hard right cut and slipped behind the pressure ridge.

My breath was coming hard and short and I could feel the cold air searing my lungs. Maybe George could go on running—maybe Mr. Marvin could do the same—but I couldn't. I jumped up onto the runners. I had to let the

dogs take me for a while. I peered past the dogs. I couldn't
see George—the route ahead was marked by high ridges—
but I could see one of the markers, glistening red in the
moonlight. Thank goodness for the moonlight.

When I'd first heard that the sun was going to set in
November and not come up again until some time in
February, I was almost afraid. I thought it would simply be
three months of darkness. But it wasn't like that. With the
high moon, midday, especially when the moon was full,
you could see clearly and see well into the distance. And
there was a full moon today. That was why the race was
being held at this time. There was enough light to see
clearly right now and there would be much more by the
time it got to noon. That was still about four hours away.
If I was lucky, if I ran hard, I could be more than halfway
through by then. That's when I'd stop for a break. Feed
and water the dogs and eat something myself as well.

I rounded another pressure ridge and in the distance
I could see George. The route ahead was straight and
flat and clear and he was so far in front of me that he
was just a tiny speck on the horizon. At least I knew I
was going the right way. I heard the sound of dogs
barking off to the side—it was Mr. Marvin! He had cut
around another ridge and was on the flat, almost paral-
lel to me! I jumped off the runners. My legs were
feeling strong and my lungs were clear. I yelled at the
dogs and, with my weight gone from the sledge, they
surged forward.

Our two sledges were coming together, both of us
heading toward the distant marker. At one point it looked
as though Mr. Marvin was ahead, then me, now we

seemed to be virtually even. His sledge slipped in beside mine. There was no more than twenty feet between us, and my lead dog was the only lead I now enjoyed. As the two teams came together the dogs started barking even louder. It was as if they were cheering each other on, or saying hello, or maybe insulting each other.

Above the din of the dogs Mr. Marvin was yelling, urging his huskies on. I began yelling at my dogs too, but it felt as though my voice was lost. Slowly his sledge started to pull away, just a little at first and then, dog by dog, his team began to get clear of mine. Finally he was obviously ahead of me. There was no point in pushing the dogs any harder. I jumped up onto the runners and eased off the reins.

Lightning kept pulling the team forward. He didn't want to give up the chase. Maybe I wanted to quit, but he didn't. I felt bad. I jumped off the runners and started yelling as loud as I could and the team surged forward.

Mr. Marvin had finally stopped running and was riding the runners. He was a big man—he had to outweigh me by sixty or seventy pounds—and his dogs would be working much harder under the additional weight. I wouldn't make my dogs work. I was going to be running until we caught him, until we *passed* him. The gap of ice between us—which had been opening up—was now becoming smaller. Mr. Marvin still hadn't noticed us gaining. It was as if he'd figured that once he'd passed I would just give up and let him go. And that might have been true . . . but neither of us had figured on Lightning. Maybe he'd underestimated both me and the dog.

We were getting closer and closer and closer and—
Mr. Marvin looked back over his shoulder. He looked
shocked to see me there. I expected him to jump off and
start running, yelling at his dogs to pull him forward.
Instead he brought one hand up to the side of this head
and saluted me! Now *I* was shocked. I just grinned and
saluted him right back!

Chapter Seventeen

I STAYED UP with Mr. Marvin for almost an hour. We talked—or really he talked and I listened. He told me things about the ice, about the Arctic. He knew a lot. He wasn't friends with any of the Eskimos, but he was always asking them questions, learning from them. He didn't see them as equals, but he did know that we were living in their world, and they knew their world much better than he did.

We travelled side by side. George had disappeared long ago and none of the others had caught up to us. We couldn't even see them, and the only dogs we could hear barking belonged to our two teams. It was almost as if we were the only two people in the world. The two of us and twenty barking huskies. The sound of barking dogs was as much a part of the Arctic to me as the wind rushing by or the noise the sledge runners made as they slid over the ice.

I stayed with Mr. Marvin as long as I could before he started to pull away. The first time that happened he yelled for me to pick up the pace. It wasn't angry yelling—he was encouraging me. I kept up with him as long as I could but eventually I knew I had to back off. I yelled for him to go on without me. Once more he gave me a salute, but this time he did something else. He yelled back, "Well done, lad, well done!"

That made me feel good inside—and a bit guilty. I wasn't falling back just because I was feeling tired and couldn't keep up. We were coming up to the marker where I would be going off course. I couldn't very well do that with him watching. How would I explain it? But maybe I should have told him and invited him to come along—maybe that would have been the sporting thing to do.

Up ahead I saw the red marker, the one that marked the place where I was supposed to cut off course. I slowed the dogs down. It looked just the way Matt had described it. There was a big pressure ridge—as big as a house. I could see the tracks of the two sledges that had gone before me shooting off to the right. This was it. I'd been counting the markers. This had to be the place—unless I'd miscounted.

I brought the dogs to a halt. Almost instantly they slumped to the ice. I walked alongside the team. They looked tired—tongues hanging out, chests heaving up and down. They needed the rest. I undid the canvas—careful not to disturb the Baby Jesus too much—to reveal the wooden box that held food for the dogs. I took off a mitt, reached in, and grabbed a piece of walrus blubber. The dogs were now all looking at me like I was the most important person in the world. Right then, I was.

I tossed the first piece toward Lightning. He leaped up into the air and grabbed it. I threw the second piece to Blackie and then a piece to each of the dogs. I then offered Lightning a second piece. He'd already devoured the first one, and besides, it was sort of like his extra pay for being in charge. After all, the captain of a ship got paid more than the third-class sailor.

There was a spot where the ridge rose up more gradually. I started up the incline. It was steep but certainly easy enough to climb . . . for me. But how hard would it be to get a team and a loaded komatik up the slope? I got to the top and looked beyond the ridge. I needed to see the way I was going to travel.

Fanning out in waves was a series of pressure ridges. They looked like a little mountain range. Matt had said they went on for about two hundred yards and that there were four or five of them, with sections of flat ice in between. All I had to do was read the compass—travel due north—until I cleared the last ridge and I came to a big stretch of flat ice. Although it was almost noon and as bright as it was going to get, there was no way I could see beyond the ridges to that flat ice. That was where I'd be back on course, having cut almost two full miles off the route.

I needed to see more. I dug in and climbed to the very top of the ridge, scanning the distance. In the direction I had come there was nobody to be seen. In the other direction, the way I should have been travelling, the way passed by Mr. Marvin and George, I couldn't see anything either. They were long gone.

Part of me wanted to simply go back to the dogs and continue on the course. Finishing third wouldn't be bad. Of course, that was assuming that nobody else would overtake me. But this way was going to cut miles of distance and at least an hour off my time. It wouldn't be that hard. As long as I went straight north it would work.

I tapped my hand against my pants pocket. I could feel my compass. It was time.

I dropped down to my bottom and slid down the pressure ridge, moving much faster than I'd come up. I slid to a stop right before slamming into the dogs. A couple of them jumped to their feet and tried to scurry away but were held in place by the lines and the weight of the other dogs. I got to my feet and brushed off the snow.

"Come on, Lightning," I said as I grabbed the dog's harness and pulled him to his feet. He willingly came with me and the rest of the team, pulling the sledge, followed along.

Lightning hesitated at the start of the slope. "Come on, boy!" I yelled and yanked on the lead. We started up. One of my feet slipped and I slumped down to all fours, releasing the lead, but Lightning kept on moving up, leading the rest of the dogs. He got to the top and then stopped. I pulled myself up and went to his side. The downward slope was steep, almost as steep as the way we'd come up. If the dogs ran fast and kept running they could get onto the flat and keep the sledge behind them. But if they stopped running then the sledge would sweep into them, smacking the last dogs in their hind legs, maybe hurting them. That was a risk I didn't want to take.

I grabbed Lightning's harness and pulled him partway down the slope. I yanked him to a stop when the sledge reached the crest. It was balanced right there on the top edge, teetering slightly. I kept a hand on the harnesses, walking back along the team until I got to the final dog. I started to untie one of the leads that connected the dogs to the sledge. The knot undid easily. That wasn't the one that worried me. Now the dogs and sledge were tied together with just one lead. One lead was stopping the sledge from going backwards down the ridge along the route we'd travelled. I needed it to come forward, but not too much or it would slide down and onto the dogs.

I nudged the last dog, and he nudged the dog in front of him and the sledge pulled a foot forward. It was now perfectly balanced. I put a foot on the sledge, holding it in place, and undid the second lead. As it dropped to the ground I felt the sledge start to slide backwards! I jumped on the front of the sledge and it tipped dangerously forward and started down the slope!

"Mush! Mush!" I yelled at the dogs.

They jumped forward a split second before I tumbled onto the sledge as it started down the slope. I tried to regain my balance but was helpless. I grabbed on, hoping it wouldn't throw me off, or tip or hit the dogs or—I bounced up in the air and landed back on top of the load as it hit the flat ice! I sat up as it slid across the ice. It had worked. The sledge was in one piece and I hadn't hit the dogs—the dogs! Where were the dogs? I turned around and burst into laughter. Lightning, leading the rest of the team, was running along behind the sledge. It looked as if they were trying to push it along. The sledge was slowing down and the dogs were starting to run alongside. Finally it came to a stop and the team stopped, almost right in front of me.

As I started to climb off the sledge I looked down. Baby Jesus was right underneath me.

"Sorry," I said, feeling stupid talking to a doll, but guilty for landing on our Saviour.

I got to my feet and grabbed the leads. I pulled Lightning forward and positioned the dogs in front of the sledge. I looped the leads around the front of the sledge, tied them off securely, and then gave the command for the dogs to pull.

THE TEAM PULLED the sledge up another slope. This had to be the last ridge. Then again, I'd thought that for the last two. We'd gone over nine pressure ridges altogether. Matt had said five—but maybe he'd meant five big ones. Some of them weren't that high, and I'd found places where I could drive the team right up and over. I was always careful when I had to move too far one way that I cut back to try to maintain a straight line. I kept checking my compass and we were heading due north. Besides the compass, I was also using the moon to guide us.

A couple of the ridges had been high and hard. There was one—I think it was the seventh—that I thought I might have to unload the sledge for, but in the end I was able to avoid that completely. I felt good about that. It wasn't just the time or work—I didn't want to disturb baby Jesus. He was sound asleep, eyes closed, perched on top of the komatik.

I'd been in the ridges and off course for a long time. I didn't have a watch but I figured it had to be at least forty minutes. It was getting close to noon and the midday moon was almost due north. This had to be the last ridge, and just on the other side of it would be the open ice and I'd be back on route. It had to be right.

I pulled at Lightning's harness and he pulled the team and the sledge forward. I slipped and put a hand down to steady myself and then got back to my feet. This was taking a lot more time and energy than I would have thought. Maybe this wasn't such a great shortcut. I could only hope that Matt knew what he was talking about.

I reached the crest of the ridge. In front of me, as far as I could see in the midday moonlight, was flat, flat ice. No ridges, nothing but open ice. I felt like yelling out loud. Instead I commanded Lightning to go down the slope. I stood there as dog after dog made the descent, then the sledge, and I grabbed onto the handles as they passed. The slope was long and gentle and I rode along. I brought the sledge to a stop at the bottom. Now I just had to turn left and keep going.

I looked ahead and behind. Nothing. Nobody. I got down low and looked for sledge tracks to see if somebody had passed by. There was almost no snow, just hard, clean ice. If somebody had already gone by I wouldn't have been able to see any telling tracks. Maybe George, or even Mr. Marvin had already passed. Maybe only George. Maybe nobody. Maybe nobody had passed this way because this wasn't the right route. That sent a chill up my spine.

Everything Matt had told me to do, the compass readings, everything said I was right where I should be. And if I was wrong? Well, if I was wrong I would know soon enough. And I'd simply turn around, climb over the pressure ridges, and go back to where I'd left the course. Then I could do one of two things: return to the race, or retrace my steps, looking for the markers, now red on my left and blue on my right, and go back to the camp. I'd be a quitter, somebody who wouldn't be going any farther, and certainly not to the Pole, but I'd be alive and safe.

Now that I had a plan I wouldn't have to think about it any more—I hoped.

The dogs had all dropped down to the ice again. This was as good a time as any to give them something more to eat. I untied the canvas and dipped into the food box. The dogs had all turned around and were watching me. I pulled out a piece of blubber and then a second and third. I tossed them to the closest three dogs and they snatched them up off the ice. There was some snarling from the next-closest dogs.

"Stop it!" I yelled. "You'll all get fed!"

I grabbed another seven pieces and held them in my arm. I walked up along the team, dropping a piece beside each dog. That would keep them satisfied for a while. My stomach growled and I realized that I'd now fed them twice but I hadn't had anything to eat myself. I walked back to the sledge and rolled the canvas farther back. There was another container that had some pemmican and jerky. The pemmican I'd save but the jerky could be eaten as I rode along. I was hungry, but more than I needed to satisfy my stomach I needed to answer my curiosity. Maybe curiosity wasn't the right word. I needed to ease my fears. There was no way I could eat until I knew we were on course. I stuffed the jerky in my pocket.

As the dogs finished off their food, I secured the lines to the sledge. They'd just been looped over and tied lightly while I was in the ridges. Now I needed them to hold firm and tight. I walked forward, yanking on each harness as I passed, pulling the dogs to their feet. Lightning didn't need to be persuaded. He was already up, waiting, pulling slightly at the leads, wanting to get moving. I started to yell out the command—before I could even finish the words Lightning had begun to move. He wanted to get running again.

I stood in place and let the team start off. As the sledge passed by I jumped on and grabbed the reins. I kept pushing with one foot, riding with the other. It wouldn't be long before I either came up to a marker or needed to turn around if I didn't. Now the moon shone brightly to my right. It was still both my light and my guide. I scanned the distance looking for that marker. It could be a red on the right or a blue on the left. It didn't matter which, I just needed one marker, something to show me that I was on course. I jumped back onto the runners. I needed to stop running so I could focus all my attention on watching for the markers.

Despite my weight the sledge was moving at a good pace. The ice was flat and smooth and fast, but it was more than that. The dogs seemed to be happy to be in harness and running. If we were on course we were making great time. If we were off course we were moving farther and farther away from safety. I had two choices. I could keep going, hoping for the best, or stop and go back, assuming the worst. But which to do? No, I had one other choice.

I pulled hard on the leads and yelled out the command for the dogs to stop. My third choice was to go no place. I had to get something to eat and drink, and the dogs needed to be watered as well. I'd wait right here. If I was on course, sooner or later somebody might simply pass by.

All of the dogs, with the exception of Lightning, had slumped down to the ice. I undid the ties holding down the canvas and pulled out the Primus stove. I was going to melt some snow for the dogs to drink. I was feeling pretty parched myself. And something to eat—something warm to eat—would warm my insides. I walked around the sledge to be on the side that was away from the wind coming off the open ice. Now that I wasn't moving I could feel the wind more. A rest would be good. Some food and water would be good. All I had to do was wait for somebody to catch me.

I STARTED at the sound of the dogs getting to their feet. Something had disturbed them. I grabbed onto the sledge and pulled myself up as well. What had they seen or heard or smelled? I looked back down the course. I couldn't see anything, but my vision was limited to maybe half a mile. Certainly not nearly as far as the dogs could see. And they could hear and smell a lot farther than that. Maybe somebody was coming.

Then again, maybe what had caught their attention wasn't coming from that direction. The wind was blowing in from off the open ice. And the ridges that ran along the other side were the perfect place to conceal a polar bear.

I reached down and grabbed the rifle that I had leaned against the side of the sledge. I had made sure to have it close at hand. Captain Bartlett had told me that the reason we had had so many polar bears come into camp was that they could pick up a scent from ten miles away. I'd been here, sitting on the ice, cooking food. If there was a polar bear anywhere around here it certainly would be coming in my direction by now. And if something was coming for me, it would be best for me to get moving again.

I leaned the rifle against the sledge again and took off my mitts. I had to tie down the load and get going. I still didn't know whether I should go forward or back but I wasn't going to sit here any longer. Then I heard something. It sounded like the distant sound of barking. I listened harder. Nothing. Maybe I was imagining it.

Lightning barked, and I was so startled I almost jumped into the air. The other dogs started yipping and barking. I tried to settle them down but they wouldn't listen. I grabbed hold of the rifle again. They had definitely sensed that something was near.

Then, down the path, I saw it—a team of dogs pulling a sledge! I felt an immense sense of relief. I felt like yelling, like laughing, like screaming, like crying. Instead I just stood there, frozen in place, watching it get bigger and bigger and closer and closer. My dogs were becoming more excited by the second and the other dogs seemed just as worked up.

I still couldn't tell who it was. Was it Mr. Marvin? Boy, would he be surprised when he saw me. Surprised and maybe angry that I'd taken a shortcut. I didn't care. He could yell at me all he wanted. It would just be good to not be alone, to know that I was in the right place, to know that I was safe.

The driver yelled for his team to slow down. Right then I recognized him. It was George! He brought the team to a stop right beside me. The dogs were all barking and yelping, calling out greetings to their friends.

"Danny," he said as he got off his sledge. "I thought you were a mirage. How in God's good name did you get here?"

"I came through the pressure ridges," I said, gesturing in that direction.

He shook his head. "Unbelievable, simply unbelievable." He took off his mitt and offered me his hand. "I must congratulate you, sir, that was a most impressive piece of navigation and, perhaps more important, courage."

I took his hand. I wanted to just let the compliment stand, but not telling him felt like a lie.

"I had some help," I said. "Matt told me there was a spot where I could go off course and gain ground."

"Perhaps he told you, but you had the strength and vision to follow that course of action." He paused. "I must admit that I am grateful to see you."

"You are?"

"I wouldn't want you to tell anybody—especially not the Commander—but I was feeling somewhat uneasy being out here by myself. It will be good to have company for the rest of the race."

"But . . . but I don't think I can keep up your pace."

"Perhaps I can slow my pace slightly. I think I'd prefer the company to the victory, or at least the sole victory. I am more than prepared to share it with you," he said. "Unless, of course, you think you can beat me to the finish line."

"No! I'd like to come along with you!"

"Good. Then let's start moving."

Chapter Eighteen

February 1, 1909

I HURRIED to pull on my mukluks, trying to walk before they were fully on and almost tripping over my own feet in the process. The Captain and Commander walked out the door and it closed behind them. I had to hurry. I pulled down my hood and reached into my pockets. My mittens weren't there. I turned back around. They were on my bunk. I wanted to just leave them there, go outside without them, but I knew the Captain would yell at me if I did. Maybe it was February 15, and practically mild compared to what the temperature had been, but it was still way below freezing and exposed skin would get frost-bitten pretty fast. I ran back and got the mitts and pulled them on.

By the time I got outside they were fifty yards away, walking toward the coast. I rushed after them. They'd told me they wanted to talk to me but they hadn't told me what they wanted to talk about. I was nervous. No, I was scared. What would they say? What had I done wrong? I had tried my best to do everything that was asked of me and—no sense in getting my guts in a knot until I knew.

I caught up and fell in right behind them. We walked in silence. Where were we going? They finally stopped on a little rise that overlooked everything. It was probably the best view for miles in any direction. Back the way we'd come was the camp. It looked so small—just a couple of dark shapes against a mass of white. There was a series of small plumes of smoke rising out of the chimneys of the building. It rose into the air and then disappeared into the gloom. To the right, over seventy miles away, safely at anchor was the *Roosevelt*. I couldn't help but wonder what it would have been like if I'd simply stayed with the ship. It certainly would have been safer, warmer, and a whole lot easier.

The two men stood, silently, looking north. I thought that they were looking toward that spot, hundreds of miles north, the Pole. I knew that Commander Peary had thought about it, dreamed about it, for so long that he *could* see it, at least in his mind.

"There it is," Captain Bartlett said.

For a split second I thought he meant the Pole. Then I saw what he was really looking at. A bright, fiery ball— the sun—was just pushing up over the horizon. The sun still hadn't risen, but we'd all noticed that it was getting brighter with each passing day. Of course, more light meant more work for those of us who were preparing, getting things ready to go.

We watched in silence as the sun continued to rise. I was amazed at how bright it was. I had to look slightly away. The entire scene became light and the sun glistened and sparkled against the snow. It was as beautiful as it was brilliant. I brought my hand up to shield my eyes. The sun was still only half up, a semicircle above the horizon. I couldn't even imagine how much brighter it was going to be when it was fully exposed. It was the most amazing thing I'd ever seen in my life. I could feel its warmth against my face. It felt so good, so welcoming, so hopeful.

And then, as quickly as it had risen, it began to set. I felt as if my heart were sinking along with it. With amazing speed it sank back into the horizon. It was as if the ice and snow were devouring it, eating the warmth. There was a mist in the distance, and I had the wildest thought that it had been caused by the snow and ice being melted when the fire of the sun was extinguished as it set. I guess I'd been listening to too many Eskimo fables. A few rays, a fainter light still remained, but the sun itself was gone. I had the urge to yell out at it, or run along the shore and try to catch it, but I just stood there and watched.

"Well, boy," Captain Bartlett said.

"It was beautiful," I said. "I could feel the warmth."

"It warmed my heart and my soul."

"Do you know what the return of the sun means?" Commander Peary asked.

"Yes, sir, that you'll be leaving soon to reach the Pole."

He chuckled softly. "I like the way you said that, son, to *reach* the Pole. Not to *try* to reach the Pole. So you think I can do it?"

"I don't think, sir, I *know*."

He placed a hand on my shoulder. "That's what I like to hear. Believing you can accomplish something is more than half the battle won. By the end of the month that five minutes that the sun rose above the horizon will become close to ten hours. Add in the time when it is light before the sun rises and after it sets there will be almost eleven hours of light. Enough to start toward the Pole. Do you know why we brought you out here?" Commander Peary asked.

"No, sir." I was feeling anxious again.

"On February the twenty-eighth, if the weather is favourable, Captain Bartlett will be leading the first party out onto the ice," Commander Peary said.

I looked over at the Captain. He had a smile that was visible through his whiskers. He looked happy at the thought.

"Others will follow, moving supplies and building shelters along the trail that Captain Bartlett will be forging. Have you given any thought to who those others might be?" he asked.

"There'll be the Eskimos. And Matthew, of course," I said.

"He will be at my side," Commander Peary said. "Who else?"

"And Mr. Marvin, and Dr. Goodsell, and Mr. MacMillan, and, of course, George."

"George has certainly shown his worth on the ice and with a team . . . as have you. You ran an outstanding race."

"Thank you, sir."

"Here is my question, Danny. Do you think that you should be coming along?" he asked.

"I'd like to come along," I said.

"That was not my question. Do you think you should be coming along?"

I didn't know what to answer to that. I felt like there was no right answer. I stood there, my mouth open, not knowing what to say.

"Don't be afraid, Danny. Nobody means ya no harm. Just answer the Commander honestly, that's all he's askin'," Captain Bartlett said.

I hesitated for a bit longer, trying to find the words to say what I wanted to say. "I guess I know the dogs as good as anybody here, except maybe the Eskimos and Matt."

"Better than Captain Bartlett?" Commander Peary asked.

I looked at the Captain, then back at the Commander, and again back at the Captain. "Yes, sir," I said softly. "I've spent more time with the dogs than he 'as and I know them dogs well."

"I think he does," Captain Bartlett said, and my fear that I'd offended him vanished. "And he certainly is willing to protect the dogs," he added. "Remember, it was 'im that went out in the middle of the night and shot that white bear. Could 'ave been a lot more dogs killed that night if not for Danny."

"Thank you for sayin' that, sir. Could I ask you a question, sir?" I asked.

"Certainly," Commander Peary said.

"No disrespect, sir, but why don't you think I should go along?"

"Your age."

"My age?"

"You're only a lad. No older than my daughter, and I certainly wouldn't want to bring her onto the ice."

I didn't know what I could say to that. I was the same age as Marie—it was a fact.

"Come now, Commander, you know it isn't the same. They're both fourteen, but bein' fourteen *and* from Newfoundland is a different thing," Captain Bartlett said. "Back home a fourteen-year-old isn't a boy, he's a man."

Commander Peary looked at me, but didn't speak. I got the feeling he was trying to see if I looked like a man. I wished I was bigger—taller or stronger—but I knew I wasn't. I looked like a boy.

"Hasn't he acted like a man?" Captain Bartlett asked.

"He has done many things that are commendable," Commander Peary said, "but none of those change his age."

"Danny," Captain Bartlett said, "let me ask you a question. I noticed you don't play with the Eskimo children. Why not? Don't you like 'em?"

"Um . . . sure . . . I guess I like them . . . I just would rather spend time with Oatah or one of the other men, that's all. I don't feel like I have a lot in common with the children."

"With them, or with any kids?" Captain Bartlett said. "How about the kids back at 'ome?"

I shook my head. "I guess I really don't play that much. I just feel . . . older."

"Then, do you feel like a man?" Commander Peary asked.

"Well, sir, I don't really know if I'm a man, but I know that I stopped being a boy the day my mother died." I paused to let those words sink in—not just for him but for me. I'd never spoken them before, never thought them before, but they were true. I had stopped being a child that day.

"'When I was a child, I spake as a child, I understood as a child, I thought as a child: but when I became a man I put away childish things,'" Captain Bartlett said.

Commander Peary nodded. "First Corinthians."

"One of my favourites," Captain Bartlett said.

"Only you, Bob, would quote the Bible to convince me of a position."

"It's called the Good Book for a reason," Captain Bartlett said.

"Well, Danny, do you have anything more you want to say?" Commander Peary asked.

"I know, sir, that if you took me along you wouldn't be making too bad a mistake."

"Actually, Danny, I'm beginning to think that if I *didn't* take you along I would be making a grave mistake." He removed his mitt and offered his hand. I ripped off my mitt and we shook.

Chapter Nineteen

February 28, 1909

I OPENED THE DOOR of the shelter. The sun hadn't quite risen above the horizon but its rays were already reflecting up and it was light enough to see into the distance. There was a grey rim across the horizon but almost no cloud cover, so there was little chance of snow, and less of a blizzard. A blizzard would be the only thing that could stop today from happening.

As I watched, the first little curve of the sun started to rise. I stood there and drank it in. It was a beautiful sight, something I looked forward to each morning. After not seeing it for almost three full months it was like a long-lost friend returning. I didn't think I'd ever take a sunrise for granted again.

As I walked toward the dogs I was surprised to see that it looked as though every single person in the compound was up and outside and waiting. There was a lot of talking and laughter, and it felt like people were waiting for a show to start, or a celebration, or maybe waiting to watch a parade. I guess it was a kind of parade. Three sledges and thirty dogs were going to be leaving, the first of many sledges that would leave over the next few days. Captain

Bartlett was leading the first group to set out—to set out for the Pole.

The sledges and the teams were at the centre of the crowd. Captain Bartlett stood beside his sledge, George at a second, and an Eskimo named Seegloo at the third. Each had ten dogs. I was happy to see that Lightning was not amongst the dogs. He wasn't mine, and I knew that, but he was my pick for lead dog. I wanted him for my sledge team. I think the Eskimos all knew and respected that. I wasn't so sure about the other members of the expedition.

I think some of the other men really resented the fact that I was being allowed to go farther. They said I was just a kid. For sure there were a lot of bad feelings hanging around because I'd beaten them in the sledge race. I'd heard some of them say that the reason I'd done so well had nothing to do with me, that it was all because of my dogs, especially my lead dog, and if they had chosen him they might have won or placed better. I'd even heard grumblings that I'd "cheated" by going off course. The Captain put those rumours down real fast. Nobody wanted to mess with the Captain. I got the feeling that even Commander Peary had such respect for him that he wouldn't go against him.

The Commander was standing beside Captain Bartlett. They had their heads close together and they were talking. Suddenly the Commander stepped up onto one of the sledges and raised his hands, signalling for silence. The crowd noise died instantly and all eyes were focused on him.

"My good and faithful friends and colleagues," he began. "We are standing here not only on the edge of the Arctic Ocean but on the edge of history. Today we begin not the first step, but the next step in our journey to the Pole. Why the Pole? It is the last great geographical prize that the world has to offer to adventurous men."

I stood there, transfixed, listening to him. Hearing him speak was like listening to music. I didn't know anybody who could make words dance the way he could.

"All of our work up to this point, all of our planning, has been designed to bring us to this moment in time. We are poised, we are now ready, to shoot forward to the Pole like a ball from a cannon!"

People cheered and clapped, and the Inuit were whistling.

I looked at the three sledges. Captain Bartlett's was different from the other two. His was practically empty while the others were piled high with supplies. That was part of the plan. The Captain would be going ahead so he could chart the route. At times he'd probably have to use his axe and pike to chop through ridges. The other two, loaded with all the supplies the three of them and their dogs would need, would follow the route that he set.

"Captain Bartlett, along with George and Seegloo, will be leading the first leg. They will be breaking the trail and marking the way for the group that will leave tomorrow, and then my party will follow the day after that. Before they depart, I would ask Captain Bartlett to say a few words."

Commander Peary stepped down and shook hands with the Captain, who took his place atop the sledge.

"I am just a small part of this expedition. I am so grateful—we all should be so grateful—to Commander Peary. Commander Peary is one of the bravest, noblest men who has ever lived, and it is my honour to serve under his command. It is his vision, his plannin', his dreams, his unwillingness to ever give up or give in to failure that allows us to stand 'ere today. It is in the name of Commander Peary that we will claim the Pole."

The crowd cheered as Captain Bartlett climbed down from his sledge. People surrounded him, shaking his hand or patting him on the back or even giving him a hug. I stood at the outside of the circle and waited until the crowd thinned out. I had something to say but I didn't want to say it in front of everybody. Finally it was just the Captain and George. I shuffled over.

"I'm gonna miss you two," I said.

"You won't be missing us for long," Captain Bartlett said. "You're heading out tomorrow along with Oatah."

"Are you nervous or excited?" George asked me.

"Both. You?"

"It'll be good to get moving again. The last few months have been like halftime in a football game. I'm ready for the second half."

I sort of understood what he meant.

"I just wanted to thank you both," I said. "Without you two I wouldn't be goin' anywhere tomorrow."

"You're comin' along because you earned the right to come along," Captain Bartlett said. "You just be sure to listen to everythin' that Oatah says. I don't want nothin' to be happenin' to ya, understand?"

"Yes, sir."

"And don't go takin' no unnecessary risks."

"No, sir. I'll just do what I'm told to do."

"Good." He offered me his hand and we shook. George gave me a pat on the back. It wouldn't be the same around here without the two of them, but with any luck I'd catch up with them in two or three days.

I watched as they returned to their sledges and did a final check, and then the Captain yelled out a command to his dogs and his team started to move. George gave me a little salute. There was a big goofy smile on his face. He looked like a little kid getting ready to open a Christmas present. He ordered his dogs to move and his sledge fell in behind the Captain's, and Seegloo's brought up the rear.

The dogs were all yapping and barking, and the dogs who weren't going along—those staked down by the shed—barked along excitedly. I'd have sworn that I could pick out Lightning's bark. He was probably upset that he wasn't going. I'd go down and see him, make sure he got an extra big meal today. I wanted him strong and ready.

I stood there, watching them drive off. They weren't just going for a short trip. They were headed for the Pole . . . *headed for the Pole*. That thought reverberated around in my head. Part of me wanted to be right there, right now, alongside the Captain. Part of me was grateful for another day before I had to leave this camp behind. Another part almost wanted to stay right here altogether. This camp wasn't much, but it had become home— another home I was going to leave behind.

The sledges got smaller and smaller until they blurred into one black line, and then a dot, and then finally

I couldn't see them at all. The Captain was gone. George was gone. Suddenly I felt less safe, more alone.

March 1, 1909

Oatah led the way. I knew that I didn't need to watch out for the markers or for open water or for polar bears. All I had to do was keep my komatik and team following his. And I made sure that I stayed right in his tracks. Open water wasn't much of a danger. Not that I'd seen any yet—but if we did, we'd just go around it. The real danger was newly frozen leads. That was places where the ice had just refrozen and it might not be thick enough to support a team of dogs and a sledge. The dogs were, of course, in a fan pattern, so if the lead dog went in the rest would be able to pull him out.

I thought back to my one fall through the ice. It might have only been three feet deep but I didn't know that at the time. I still had nightmares about it. For me it was scary, terrifying, before it just became silly and embarrassing. But if I fell through the ice here it wouldn't be three feet deep, it would be three *thousand* feet deep. Captain Bartlett had told me they had done soundings, measuring the depth of the water, and they couldn't even find the bottom in some places along here.

I started looking at the ice between Oatah's sledge and mine. I knew this was silly. If he had passed over it, weighed down with more supplies than I was carrying, then it would hold me. I kept looking anyway.

Just off to my right a red marker appeared. This one was a pole hammered into the ice with a small patch of brightly coloured cloth attached as a flag. In some places they had been dropping off the pemmican cans, tipping them up on their sides. In other places you could tell we were on track because the team ahead had had to hack through pressure ridges, cut a path wide enough to get the sledge through. It was reassuring whenever we came across something that showed they'd been that way and we were following behind. Oatah was a good guide, and I was told that the Eskimos could track a sledge even if there weren't any markers left. Still, there was something good about seeing the markers with my own eyes. I really liked the poles. It was like the little flags were waving hello and then goodbye. As well, the little burst of colour was a welcome relief from the relentless white of the ice and snow.

Oatah was slowing down. We'd been travelling hard for almost four hours but he had only stopped once, and that was over two hours ago. We were due for a break, weren't we? He brought his team to a halt and I jumped up on the runners to slow my team down. As I looked ahead I saw why he had stopped. There was an igloo!

I pulled hard on the leads and the dogs went to a walk and then stopped right behind his sledge. The team behind me did the same.

"An igloo?" I asked, pointing out the obvious. "Why is there an igloo?"

"Captain Bob stopped here last night," Oatah said.

"Here? Why wouldn't they have gone farther?" I asked.

He gave me a strange look. "As far as he could go."

"But it only took us four hours to get here," I said.

"Captain *break* trail. We *follow* trail."

That made perfect sense. We'd glided through pressure ridges that they'd had to hack through. Of course we'd been able to move faster.

"Do we stay here?"

Oatah laughed. "Dogs . . . water . . . food. Then go on."

Oatah started to undo the canvas to get the food for the dogs. I was tired, thirsty, and hungry, but I knew that the dogs came first. I went back to my sledge to take care of the huskies, as did the third member of our party, Ookeah. He didn't talk much, even to the other Eskimos, but he was always friendly and smiling.

The dogs were all lying down, but they roused when I started to undo the canvas. They knew there was a chance they were going to get fed. The majority of the weight on the sledge was food for the dogs. They were working hard and had to be well fed to do that work. I grabbed a piece of walrus blubber and tossed it toward the huskies. They briefly fought over it before one of the bigger dogs claimed it. I grabbed an armful and made sure that each dog had at least one piece—and Lightning a second.

I had eaten blubber, but this stuff looked like it was turning bad. The dogs didn't seem to mind. I figured the huskies would eat pretty much anything that was given to them, including your fingers if you weren't careful.

As I finished, I noticed that Ookeah was unloading his sledge and bringing things over to the igloo. Why was he doing that? I thought about asking him but figured it would be better to ask Oatah. He was just finishing with his team.

"Oatah?" I asked, gesturing to Ookeah.

"Unload. Go back."

"We're going back?" I exclaimed.

"*Ookeah* go back. We go," he said pointing in the direction we had been driving.

"Oh . . . so we keep going." That was good . . . at least I thought it was good.

I knew that our job was to bring out supplies, ferry them out onto the ice, but I just thought that we'd all be staying together. I sort of wanted all of us to stay together, but as long as I was with Oatah I'd be safe. Besides, if we continued at this pace—and Captain Bartlett had moved at the same pace today as yesterday—we might catch him before the day ended.

"My dogs are ready to go and so am I," I said to Oatah. "Can we leave?"

"Soon, soon. Not tired?"

"Not any more." The thought of catching the Captain had eased the strain in my legs.

Oatah didn't say anything more. He walked over to his sledge and started to tie down the canvas. I did the same.

WE'D BEEN TRAVELLING less than an hour when I began to regret leaving so quickly. Oatah was setting a fast pace, faster than I could keep up for very long. I wanted to ask him to slow down, and I knew he would if I asked him, but I couldn't do that. I had to try to stay up with him.

The ice had been mostly flat and clear. That meant that we weren't gaining much time or distance on the Captain and the others. Depending on how fast they were travelling we might actually be falling farther behind. I knew how fast George and the Captain could move. Only the Eskimos were faster. Then again, the pace Oatah was setting was as fast as anybody's, and I was keeping up with him. I felt a swell of pride. I *did* deserve to be out here. Right then, running along beside the sledge, I made a decision. I was going to prove to everybody that it had been the right choice for me to come along. I wouldn't complain, and I wouldn't stop, even if I thought my legs were going to drop off and my lungs were on fire. And just then—right up ahead Oatah stopped. I slowed my dogs down and came to a halt right beside him.

He was perched up on his sledge, standing on his toes, staring and pointing into the distance. I tried to see what he was seeing but couldn't.

"What, what is it?" I asked anxiously.

He pointed again. I saw nothing but white in all directions. I strained my eyes. I could see, or thought I could see, a big pressure ridge up ahead.

"See?" Oatah asked.

I nodded. "Sure." That must have been what he was looking at.

"Komatik," he said.

I started. I looked back toward the ridge. If there was a sledge there I certainly couldn't see it.

Oatah yelled out a command to his dogs and his team surged away. I started after him, following right in his tracks—the safest place to be.

I almost couldn't believe that he had seen something I couldn't, but I knew he had Eskimo eyes and I had white eyes. He had helped me learn to pick things out, but I'd never be able to see like an Eskimo. He probably had seen a sledge . . . wait . . . *a* komatik? Didn't he mean komatiks, like *three*? Maybe it was just a language thing and he didn't know about plurals. No, he always said *dogs,* not *dog*. If he saw just one komatik, what did that mean about the other two?

I jumped up on my sledge, rising up on my toes to look as far into the distance as I could. I scanned the horizon. I still couldn't see anything. I jumped back down and started running. My legs were feeling heavy, but my curiosity was stronger than my sense of tiredness. Besides, if he really did see something we wouldn't have to run very far. I yelled out at the dogs to run harder and I did the same as they surged forward.

I kept my eyes on my dogs. I couldn't waste energy trying to see what was ahead and where we were going. I just had to put one foot after the other, step after step, keep going and keep up with Oatah. He knew where we were going. I only had to know where *he* was going.

Five minutes turned into ten, and then ten to twenty. We were still running. If he had really seen something, surely we would have reached it by now.

We were getting closer to the pressure ridge. It was a big one. It was hard to tell distances or size up here, especially without anything to compare things to, but I could see that it was pretty high and stretched from one side to the other, disappearing in the distance in both directions. Had they hacked their way through the ridge or had they gone around it? And if they'd gone around, in what direction? I guess we'd find out pretty soon.

The dogs started to bark louder. They'd seen something too. I jumped back onto the runners and looked past Oatah. There it was! A sledge and a team of dogs! There was a figure out on the ice, waving his hands over his head. We were still too far away to tell who it was, but I could see there was only *one* figure. Three had set out. Where were the other two?

We got closer and closer. Who was it? I really couldn't tell . . . then I heard a voice calling out above the racket of the dogs. It was George! He was jumping up and down and waving and hooting and calling. Even if I hadn't heard the voice I'd have known it was George. I couldn't imagine the Captain or one of the Eskimos acting that way.

"Oatah! Danny! Good to see you lads!" George called out.

"It's good to see you, but the Cap'n . . . Seegloo . . . where are they?"

"One went that way and the other went that way," he said, pointing in both directions along the pressure ridge. "Too tall to scale or chop through so they're looking for a way around."

That was a relief. "How long have they been gone?" I asked.

"Close to two hours. When one of them finds a way around he'll come back. They left me here to build an igloo," he said, gesturing to a pile of snow blocks that had collapsed onto itself.

I started to laugh.

"Can't blame you," George said. "Pretty pathetic. Oatah, can you help build an igloo?"

Oatah nodded his head. "Danny . . . dogs."

"And while Danny is caring for the dogs I'll unload your sledges," George said. "This will be the second stepping stone, the second cache of supplies. Hopefully we'll be all settled in by the time the Captain returns."

Chapter Twenty

March 2, 1909

I WOKE with a start, my heart racing, not knowing where I was. It was pitch-black and I couldn't see . . . and then I remembered. I was in the igloo. Sleeping beside me were George and Oatah. The Captain hadn't returned, and neither had Seegloo. George and Oatah had told me not to worry. All that had happened was that night had arrived before they could return and they had made camp for the night somewhere out on the ice. The Captain could make an igloo almost as well as the Eskimos. He'd be fine. They'd all be fine. And tomorrow they'd both return. One, or maybe both of them had found a route around the pressure ridge. Then the three of them would continue on and Oatah and I would go back, get more supplies, and bring them farther along the route. No problem. Nothing to worry about.

But I was still worried.

It had to be close to morning. At least I hoped it was. It hadn't been a very good night's sleep. I was continually woken up by the sounds of the ice. I'd slept onboard ship many times and was used to the noise that a ship made—the creaking and grinding of timbers—but this was different.

The ice made sounds that could be almost lulling, almost gentle and relaxing. It could be a gurgle, or a sound like a mumbling voice, or even a crackling like the sound a fire makes. But then, every now and again, the sound would explode, like a gunshot or a door slamming. I'd be jarred fully awake, scared that the ice was opening up close by or even right under our heads. Then there'd be nothing, and the loudest sound would be the snoring coming from Oatah. If he was sleeping right through it, how much danger could there be? I'd put my head back down and try to sleep again . . . until the next loud, unexpected sound that might signal the ice opening up.

That was the great danger. I'd heard enough stories from both the Eskimos and Captain Bartlett and Matt about leads opening up practically right under your feet. Matt even told a story about a lead opening up in the middle of an igloo while men were sleeping in it. Just like this igloo. That was the story that spooked me the most. Out on the ice you could see a lead coming, you could back off or leap over it. In an igloo you could be trapped, the lead separating you from the door, or maybe all the ice falling on you and pinning you down or—I suddenly felt like the little room was becoming smaller, like I was having trouble drawing in breath. I had a feeling like I was suffocating. I had to go outside.

I sat up and felt around, trying to locate the fasteners so I could do up my parka. Despite the fact that the only thing between me and the ice was a single skin, and we were in a shelter made of ice, I had been feeling so warm that I'd unfastened the front of my jacket and taken off my mitts and hat, which I'd been using for a pillow. I pulled them on. The next part would be trickier. I had to get by Oatah to make it to the opening.

I got to my feet, but stayed crouched over so I didn't hit my head on the little ice dome. I took a big step, big enough I hoped to step over his sleeping form. He continued to snore. I went back down to my knees and moved the little curtain that was blocking the opening. I dropped on my belly and started to slide through. I hesitated.

I thought about how polar bears stood over top of a little hole in the ice, one paw poised in the air, waiting for a seal to stick its head up so it could be dispatched with one powerful chop. What would a polar bear think of this little hole in the ice? Would he think it was any different? I could just picture a big white sitting on his haunches waiting for me to stick my head up and—no, that made no sense. If there was a bear anywhere near here the dogs would be going wild. I pushed through the opening.

The sun still hadn't risen but it was light enough to see into the distance. The moon was full and low on the horizon and throwing off light from one direction. In the other, to the north, I could see where the sun's rays were being reflected up from below the horizon. It probably wouldn't be much longer until the sun rose completely.

The seasons were changing so fast now that we were getting almost fifteen minutes more sunlight every day.

That was great for travelling. Unfortunately, it also signalled our need to travel faster. More sun, more warmth; the more warmth, the less stable the ice was. There was only a certain amount of time to get to the Pole. Captain Bartlett called it a window opening before the door slammed shut in our faces. I thought that was a pretty silly way of saying it, but I knew what he meant. If the Pole wasn't reached by a certain date, it wouldn't be reached at all.

The dogs were all lying on the ice, curled up in little balls, their tails covering their faces. Some had chosen to sleep in groups, two or three dogs in a ball. That was for affection as much as it was for warmth. Lightning saw me and stood up. Other dogs followed. I thought they might be anxious to get moving again. Either that or they were hoping for breakfast. Maybe I could sneak a little something to my team.

All at once all of the dogs seemed to wake up. They got to their feet and started moving. Had I done that? Had I disturbed them? No, they weren't paying attention to me. They all seemed to be facing the other direction, staring, ears perked up, listening. What had they seen or heard?

I hurried over to my sledge. I pulled back the canvas and lifted up the rifle. Maybe nothing. Maybe a bear. Better to be prepared and have nothing happen than not be prepared and have something happen. I pulled back the bolt and fed a bullet into the chamber and then walked over to the dogs. All thirty were on their feet, ignoring me, staring into the distance. Whatever they'd seen or heard was beyond my ability to detect. I pulled off my hat and turned my head to see if I could hear something. There was the wind, but nothing else. The wind—maybe that was it. It was blowing from the direction they were staring. Maybe it was a smell. Oatah had told me that the dogs had noses like the bears and could smell things from dozens of miles away. If it was a bear they were smelling, I hoped it *was* a dozen miles away.

"What is it?"

I spun around and jumped into the air and—

"Whoa, watch where you're aiming that rifle!" It was George. He had grabbed the end of my rifle and was pushing it away.

"I'm sorry . . . you startled me!" I exclaimed, feeling embarrassed. "I didn't hear you!"

"I'm sorry I startled *you*," he said as he took the rifle from my hands. I surrendered it willingly. "You more than startled me when you pointed that rifle at me. I was just checking on you. I saw you leave the igloo. Why are you out here?"

"Just wanted some air . . . and then the dogs noticed something . . . I don't know, but I think there's something out there. Maybe a bear, that's why I had the rifle."

"A bear would be good," George said.

"It would?"

"If we kill a bear that would be food for two weeks or more for a whole team of dogs. That's like a fully loaded sledge that wouldn't have to be brought out."

"I hadn't thought of that."

"You should. Could save a lot of work for somebody, maybe for you."

I was going to answer him when I thought I heard something. I turned my head to the side to try to capture the sound. At the same instant the dogs started to make little whining sounds. They had heard something too. I had to fight the urge to reach over and take my rifle back, but if there was a bear coming it would be better if it was in George's hands.

"Whatever it is, it's coming from that direction," George said.

He had to be right. Every single dog was standing, facing in the same direction, like little compasses aimed north.

"Here," George said and handed me the rifle. "I'm going to get Oatah . . . and my rifle."

I was glad to have the rifle in my hands and glad that Oatah was going to be joining us, but a bit uneasy about being left alone, even for a minute. I scanned the horizon in the direction the dogs were staring. I couldn't see anything. That was good. At least I guessed that was good. My eyes weren't sharp like the Eskimos', but even I would have seen a polar bear lumbering toward us. Oatah would be here soon. If there was something out there he'd see it. Forget about somebody having eyes like an eagle—what they really needed were eyes like an Eskimo.

One of the dogs yipped and I started again. I was glad I didn't have my finger on the trigger or I might have fired a round into the air accidentally. Another dog joined in and then another and another until all thirty dogs were barking in a very out-of-tune chorus. If George hadn't woken Oatah already he'd be awake now. The dogs continued to bark. It wasn't angry. There was no snarling or growling. It sounded like the noises they made when they were running, encouraging each other, or when they saw another team and were welcoming them. Could that be it? Did they think there was another team?

I focused my gaze on the base of the pressure ridge. I allowed my eyes to follow it along, moving my head slowly to see farther and farther and—I stopped. There was a black mark, almost like a deeper shade or shadow against the darkness of the ridge. I blinked and it was still there. What was it? And more important, was it moving this way? Was it getting bigger? I stood frozen in place, watching.

"Do you see something?" George asked. He and Oatah were standing beside me, rifles in hand.

I turned back toward the spot—I hoped I hadn't lost it. I focused my eyes and there it was. "Out there," I said, pointing. "Against the pressure ridge."

"I don't see anything," George said. "Where is it?"

"Right there. Follow my arm with your eyes until your gaze hits the ridge."

He moved over so he was standing right beside me. He looked, stared into the distance. "I don't see anything. Are you sure there's something out there?"

"Positive, it's right there. I think it's comin' toward us."

"Komatik and team," Oatah said.

"It is?" George asked.

He nodded. "One man, one komatik, team of dogs. Danny got good eyes."

"Thanks," I said, although my eyes certainly weren't as sharp as his. To me it just looked like a dark shadow.

"You can see all of that?" George asked.

"It is Captain Bob," he said.

"You can tell it's Cap'n Bartlett?" I exclaimed. Just how good were his eyes?

"Has to be. Coming from there," he said.

Of course, that only made sense. Seegloo had gone off the other way, so if it was a sledge coming from that direction it would have to be the Captain. It wasn't like we were going to run into strangers travelling across the polar ice.

"I'm going to send out a greeting," George said.

He pointed his rifle up and shot into the air. For a split second the dogs all stopped barking . . . and then they began again even louder. A few more seconds passed and then there was an answering shot—much softer, but definitely the sound of a gun.

"How far away is he?" I asked.

"Hard to say," George said. "Distances are so hard to judge out here."

I looked at Oatah. "How far is he?"

He gave me a confused look and then gestured out in the distance. "That far."

"I meant, how many miles or . . . " I figured this probably wouldn't work. "Do I have time to put on some coffee before he comes?"

He nodded his head.

"I'll take care of that," George said. "I'd like something warm in my stomach myself."

Oatah stood right beside me and we watched. There was no talking. I'd learned that about the Eskimos.

They were friendly and everything but they didn't waste words. If there was nothing to say they didn't say anything.

As we watched the little blob of dark grow in size and shape, the sun rose above the horizon and the scene became bright. I could now clearly see the sledge, team and man. They closed in so I could hear those dogs answering back the calls of the dogs in the camp—which kept getting louder and more excited. Finally I could tell it was Captain Bartlett. I waved and he waved back. The sledge glided into the camp and he came to a stop right beside us.

"Hello, Cap'n, it's good ta see you!" I exclaimed.

"Could'a fooled me," he said. "Were you two planning on shooting me?" he asked, gesturing to the rifles in our hands.

I started to answer when I realized that of course he was joking. "Did you find a way around the ridge?"

He nodded. "The ridge goes on for as far as I could go, at least ten miles, but I did find a place through it. Chopped it out last evenin' before I built my shelter for the night."

"That's what George said you'd do."

As we talked, without anybody asking, Oatah had untied the dogs from the sledge and was leading them away, undoubtedly to be fed and watered.

"George is puttin' on coffee," I said. He was over by the sledges and had started the little Primus stove.

"Coffee will warm my stomach and my soul. Good to see you and Oatah. Good to see George is fine. Has Seegloo returned?"

"Not yet, but we didn't expect ya back this soon. Sun's hardly up."

"No time to waste. We'll eat an' get the dogs tended to and then George and me have to be off again."

"And me and Oatah?"

"You wait for Seegloo to return. When he does, send him along after us. Then the two of you head back."

"We're goin' back?" I exclaimed. I didn't want to go back, I wanted to go farther and—

"You have to. Those supplies aren't gonna be movin' up by themselves. You'll load up again and follow behind us. If all goes well, you'll catch us in three or four days."

Chapter Twenty-One

MY SLEDGE WAS EMPTY except for a change of clothing and my rifle. Oatah had a skin tent, his rifle, and one
day's supply of food for us and the dogs. The rest had been
left behind at the second igloo. It was amazing how fast we
were moving now that the sledges weren't weighed down.
Not only were we moving fast but I could mostly ride
along, pushing with one foot, and we could still make
good time.

It seemed as though the dogs were excited about
heading back. Me, I was feeling sort of mixed up inside
about the whole thing. It would be good to sleep back
on land and not worry about the ground opening up
underneath me, but I didn't want to spend any more
than one night on land before we headed back out.
I didn't want to let the Captain get that much farther
ahead of me. It would also be tough to be moving a
fully loaded sledge again after this trip, but that was the
price I'd have to pay to come back.

Oatah was, of course, leading the way, so I wasn't
paying any attention to the route. I'd seen one marker—
almost by accident—but nothing else. I knew we were on
course, but still, it would have been reassuring to see
another marker or two. Or to reach the first igloo. That

would mark time and distance. It would also mean that if a storm did come—and there was no sign on the horizon—we'd have a ready-built shelter and enough supplies to last for days and days.

Of course there was one other thing that might happen before we reached the igloo—we could meet with another party heading out onto the ice. I wanted to meet another party, but I had a competition going on in my mind: I wanted to get to the first igloo before they got there coming from the other direction. It was a race—a race where I was the only one who was aware that it was happening.

I jumped off the runners and started running behind the sledge. I yelled for the dogs and they responded instantly. We began to move up. I got the feeling that Lightning wasn't ever happy being behind another team and wanted to get in front of those other dogs. We started to pull up, closer and closer, and then Oatah's team started running faster and pulled away again. Oatah hadn't given them the command to pick up the pace, it was just that their lead dog didn't want to be beaten either. That was all right. As long as we were moving faster, I was happy.

WE GLIDED TO A STOP beside the igloo. I hadn't noticed it until we were practically right there, but I was so glad to see it. It was almost noon. We'd been moving for almost five hours and I was hungry and thirsty and tired. We could eat and also feed and water and rest the dogs.

Almost the instant that the sledges came to a stop Oatah was undoing the canvas to get out the food. Not the food for us, but for the dogs. The dogs always came first. That struck me as a little strange, if you considered that if there wasn't any food for us the dogs might *become* food. Then again, maybe that made perfect sense. You wanted them to be in good shape if you ever had to eat them. I knew that wasn't the reason. The dogs weren't just transportation. They were survival. Without them the Eskimos couldn't hunt.

The dogs were settled into the snow and eagerly awaiting their meal. Oatah tossed the first piece to his lead dog and then the second to Lightning. I grabbed other pieces and soon all the dogs were happily chewing. He then broke out some jerky and some pemmican for us. Oatah crouched down and I sat on the snow beside him.

I looked at the igloo. The entrance had been sealed up with snow. That was to keep the smells in and the polar bears and Arctic foxes out. If we needed anything we'd have to dig the tunnel out again. But we weren't going to do that. We would be back at the camp within three or four hours—maybe less—because we were going to be carrying almost nothing and the dogs would all be running at top speed.

Oatah abruptly rose to his feet and pointed into the distance. I scrambled up as well, wondering what he'd seen. I'd taken a step toward the sledge to get my rifle when I heard something and turned around. It was faint, but I could hear it. The distant sound of dogs, barking and baying, carried by the wind.

I let my eyes trail out away from where we stood in the direction we would be travelling. It had to be coming from there. Slowly, Eskimo style, I let my eyes trail the path and—there it was! There were teams . . . one . . . two . . . three teams moving toward us . . . no wait, there was a fourth team, well behind the others. I wondered who was there. I wondered who it was that we'd beaten to the igloo.

I still wanted to go and get the rifle. Not to protect us, but to fire a welcoming shot into the air. But I didn't. Instead I took a bite of the jerky. Whether they were coming or not, I was still hungry. The jerky was tough and salty but tasted good. That probably said more about how hungry I was than how delicious it actually was. These past few days everything tasted good—even pemmican—and I couldn't seem to get enough. I was always hungry. I guess that made sense. It wasn't just that I was working so hard, running and moving supplies, but also because of the cold. My body needed food to keep warm, the way a house needs extra logs in the furnace in the winter.

It was funny about the cold. After a while you just didn't feel it any more. I knew it was cold—frigid—but you just became numb to it. Maybe it was the way you didn't notice air unless there was a wind, or the way a fish probably wasn't aware of water unless there was a current.

Oatah stood beside me and looked at the incoming sledges.

"Who is it?" I asked.

"Ookeah . . . *Miy Paluk* . . ."

That was Matt! That could mean only one thing. "Commander Peary, too?"

Oatah nodded. "And Dr. Goodsell."

One of our dogs howled and that ignited the others. Almost instantly there was a chorus of barking, and the teams coming answered back. I'd gotten to like the sound of the animals. I almost wanted to give a howl myself as a way of welcoming the party.

As they closed in I could see that three of the sledges were loaded down with supplies. The fourth—the one piloted by Commander Peary—was much more lightly loaded. Because of his toes—or I guess lack of toes—the Commander had trouble running along with the team and spent most of his time riding on the runners. He wasn't a little man and his weight meant that the sledge couldn't handle much else. It was strange, he was the leader of the party, the one who decided who should go along, which people were the best sledge drivers, but he was probably the worst of everybody. It wasn't that he didn't know how to drive, or control the dogs, and he could even speak to them in Inuktitut, but it was the way he moved. Or really, didn't move. And because of that he couldn't bring supplies to care for himself and his team. He had to rely on somebody else to take care of his needs.

Ookeah came into camp first, followed by Matt and the Commander. Dr. Goodsell was still well in the distance— at least a minute or two back.

"Good afternoon, gentlemen!" Commander Peary yelled out, as he waved a greeting.

"Good afternoon to you too, sir!" I called back.

All three sledges came to a stop. Ookeah started to care for the dogs. Oatah looked as though he was about to help when the Commander stopped him.

"Tell me, what is ahead?" he asked.

"Ice open."

"Straight line north?" Commander Peary asked.

Oatah nodded. "Rest of day, then pressure ridge, go," he said, pointing off to the west. "Big ridge."

"But the Cap'n found a way through it," I added.

"Captain Bob would find a way through. How far ahead are they?" he asked.

"They left at the same time as us," I said, "moving north while we moved south, so they're eight hours by sledge north of here."

"Good. If we go with speed we'll catch them by midday tomorrow."

"A train only moves as fast as the last car," Matt said. He gestured out onto the ice where Dr. Goodsell was still off in the distance.

"That does present some difficulty," Commander Peary agreed. "There is only one possible solution." He turned to me and Oatah. "Have you two eaten?"

"Just some jerky," I said.

"Then you will dine with us. Matt, please prepare food for the party."

"Yes, sir."

"I can help," I said and started off.

"Not necessary," Commander Peary said. "Matt is a very able servant. He'll fix us a warm meal, while Ookeah tends to the dogs."

"And what should we do, sir?"

"Take your personal possessions from your sledges and unhook your teams."

"You want our teams?" I exclaimed. I didn't want to give up my team, especially not Lightning.

"No, *you* will want your teams. Oatah will hook his team onto the sledge that Ookeah has brought out, and when Dr. Goodsell arrives, you, Danny, will be driving his sledge with your team."

I understood the words, but I didn't understand what he meant. Why did he want us to do this?

"The Doctor and Ookeah will bring your empty sledges back to the base camp and you two will be accompanying Matthew and me on the next stage."

OATAH AND MATT took turns leading. Commander Peary came next, and I brought up the rear. I could have easily passed the Commander. Despite having an almost empty sledge, he still wasn't able to move that fast. It made me realize just how slow Dr. Goodsell had been if he couldn't even keep pace with the Commander. I had had some vague thoughts that if we moved fast enough we might have overtaken George and the Captain before nightfall, but that just wasn't going to be happening. At this pace, it would take us most of the remaining light just to get back to where Oatah and I had started the day.

I had begun to be more aware of the ice beneath us. The passage of all those sledges had scarred the surface. I was able to pick out our trail now. It might not have been obvious to everybody—well, to everybody who wasn't an Eskimo—but it was certainly noticeable.

What was also noticeable was the way the wind had picked up. It was strong and coming almost straight out of the north, directly into our faces. It was bitter and blew snow and ice at us. I kept my head tilted slightly down, protected by the rim of the hood of my parka and partially blocked by the load on the sledge.

When I had been offered the opportunity to come along with Matt and the Commander, the chance to catch George and the Captain, I'd been thrilled. That thrill had long since gone and been replaced by the ache in my legs, the biting wind in my face, and the nervous feeling in my guts. I really didn't want to sleep out on the ice again. Especially not in that same igloo. Something about that igloo just bothered me.

Chapter Twenty-Two

March 3, 1909

THE SUN WAS SO WARM, so good. I could feel it against my skin, radiating inward, warming my body and my soul. I felt like a cat, lying close to the stove, drinking in the heat. Maybe I could go for a swim and—

"Everybody up! Everybody out!"

I started awake, confused, stunned, and unable to see anything in the pitch-black of the igloo. Somebody grabbed me by the shirt and pulled me to my feet! There was yelling and screaming but the voices were almost drowned out by a roaring, crashing sound coming from outside. And then suddenly I was hit in the side of the head, staggered, almost fell over—the roof was collapsing on our heads! There was more light, but the roar was even louder—what was happening? I stumbled over the remaining blocks and fell over the walls and out of the igloo. Oatah was on one side and Matt on the other—he had a grip on my parka, he was the person who'd pulled me to my feet. Commander Peary stumbled out of the remains of the igloo. Awkwardly he shuffled over to us.

As instantly as it had started the noise just stopped. We stood there, in complete silence, a million pinprick stars overhead and a bright, bright moon providing the light by which we could see the shattered igloo. In panic and confusion I looked at Matt. He looked calm. That suddenly made me feel calmer.

"Almost broke underneath our heads," Commander Peary said.

Then I saw it. A large ridge of ice had piled up just over from the igloo. And right in front of it, right up against the wall, was a gash, an open river of water. My mouth dropped open in shock. I was dreaming about going for a swim and that dream had almost turned into a nightmare.

"The dogs, where are the dogs?" Matt asked.

I snapped back to reality. The dogs were tied down to the ice beside the entrance to the igloo . . . the entrance that was now almost in the open water . . . oh my God . . . the dogs were gone . . . Lightning was gone!

"Lightning!" I yelled, and ran toward the open water.

Matt grabbed me and practically yanked me off my feet.

"Lightning!" I yelled. "Lightning!"

"He's gone, Danny. They're all—"

There was a bark, and a second one, and howling, and then we could hear a whole choir of dogs barking and yelling!

"They must be on the other side of the ridge. They're alive!" I yelled.

"At least some of them," Matt said, curbing my excitement. Was Lightning alive? Was Blackie okay?

"Matthew, Danny, Oatah, go and get the dogs," Commander Peary ordered.

The gash and the pressure ridge were long. They extended into the distance in one direction as far as the eye could see. In the other, the ridge and open water were stopped at the massive pressure ridge to our right, the ridge that had forced the Captain to go around. The ridge that had stopped us before was now our route to the dogs.

"Come on!" I yelled, and I started running.

"Slow down, Danny! Wait!" Matt called after me, but I kept going.

I reached the ridge and started to climb. It was then, as I put my hands down to gain traction, that I realized I wasn't wearing any mitts. I dug into my pockets. There was one but not two. I put it on and kept going. I wanted to get high enough to at least see over that smaller ridge, to see the dogs. I didn't need to get to them right away but I needed to know they were all there. I scrambled up the ridge, digging in with my feet and clawing with my hands—the hand without the mitt could actually grip better.

"Take more care!" Matt yelled.

I heard his words but needed to see the dogs. I kept climbing and—I saw the first dogs! They had broken free from the ice but were still all tied together as a team. It wasn't my team. There was a sledge . . . a second sledge . . . and a few dogs, loose, but I couldn't see any more, my view was still blocked by the ridge.

"I can see some of the dogs!" I yelled down to the rest of the party. Matt and Oatah were following behind me.

I had to climb higher to see more. I dug in deeper and climbed up over another chunk of ice and another and tried to look over and—my foot slipped and I almost tumbled down. I needed to focus on the climbing.

I reached and pulled myself up to another layer and
stopped. I could see more dogs, another team, still all
tied together but loose, and a third sledge . . . but no
Lightning. I couldn't see my team!

"Lightning!" I yelled out. "Lightning!"

There was an answering bark that rose above the rest
of the noise—was that him? I started to climb, and then
I saw him—Lightning! He had poked his head over the
top of the little pressure ridge. He climbed higher, and
then I could see that he was dragging the rest of my team
along with him!

"They're all okay!" I called back down the trail.
"I think they're all there! The dogs are fine!"

IT TOOK US A WHILE to corral the dogs that had
gotten loose. They had been spooked by the ice being
ruptured, and they didn't seem to want to be put back in
harness. I couldn't blame them. I was feeling pretty
spooked too, and I wasn't sure how I was going to sleep
tonight. The last place I wanted to be was in an igloo on
the ice . . . no . . . the last place I wanted to be was in the
water, *underneath* an igloo.

Oatah had been leading this whole leg. Commander
Peary followed, then me, and Matt brought up the rear.
The komatiks had been knocked around as well by the
shifting ice, and one of them had been damaged. Oatah
had repaired the damaged komatik and Matt had
rearranged the load. At first I couldn't see what he was
doing, and then it became more obvious. He was putting
most of the heavy things on the sledges that belonged to
him and Oatah. They were making the load lighter for me.

I told him he didn't need to do that, that I could pull my own weight, but he told me he was in charge. I felt bad at first—I really wanted to do my share—but now that we were moving, I was just grateful.

"Whoa!" Oatah called out, and his team came to a stop. Peary pulled up behind him and then I brought my sledge to rest. Finally Matt came in behind me.

Oatah pointed up into the pressure ridge. There was a trail gouged through the ice. It was marked by poles and pemmican cans so it couldn't be missed. The trail was narrow—it looked barely wide enough to allow a sledge to pass—and it was on a steep incline.

"Danny, unhook your team from the sledge," Commander Peary ordered.

"Yes, sir." I wanted to ask why, but I knew it wasn't my place to question. I hurried to follow his direction.

Matt offered his assistance. I could ask Matt.

"What's happening?"

"We're going to double-team," he said. "The only way to get through that gap is to put twenty dogs on each sledge to get them over the ridge. Your team is with me. You'll be driving."

"Me? You want me to drive?" I exclaimed. I couldn't believe my ears. Matt was a much better driver than me, a much better driver than anybody, even better than some of the Eskimos.

"Unless you want to be pulling them from the front," he said.

"Pulling them?"

"The dogs won't want to go through the gap . . . too narrow . . . the walls are all closed in. The dogs don't like to be closed in or crowded. Besides, you won't be so much driving the sledge as pushing it. You'll see."

Matt took Lightning's lead and brought my team over to his. He lined them up so he could tie my dogs to the front of his team. As he started to position them, his lead dog lunged and tried to bite one of my dogs! My husky jumped forward, barely escaping the snapping jaws! Matt yelled at his dog and it dropped to the ice in a submissive pose.

I knew his lead dog. He was big and strong and one of the dogs I always avoided because I didn't think that I could trust him. One minute he was all friendly and wagging his tail and the next he was trying to bite off your fingers. He was wagging his tail now, and pushing his head against Matt's hand to get rubbed. Obviously the dog knew that Matt was in charge. He allowed the other dogs to be tied on in front of him.

Matt walked to the front of the double-team and I went to the back of the sledge. He put one hand on Lightning's lead and then pulled him forward while he commanded the whole team to follow. He led them up the incline and into the gap. There was a slight hesitation but the dogs kept moving. Quickly the walls of ice rose up until I couldn't see over them. The sides of the sledge bounced against the ice. If I hadn't known that the Captain had carved this out and passed this way I wouldn't have thought it was possible to get through.

We slowed to a stop as the sledge ground against the ice. Matt yelled out to the dogs and I pushed as hard as I could and we popped through the gap and kept moving. This happened again and again. I could feel sweat dripping down my chest—it was hard work, much harder than driving a sledge and team along the open ice. How much farther did we have to go?

I pulled myself up and looked beyond the sledge, the dogs, and Matt. I could see that the path continued to rise up, that we hadn't reached the highest point, so I had to assume we hadn't reached the halfway mark, either.

There was barking from behind me. I turned. Oatah was leading a second double-team. They were pulling Commander Peary's almost empty sledge. I knew that no matter how hard I was working Oatah would be working harder because the Commander wouldn't be able to push much—he'd basically be pulled along by the dogs and Oatah.

The sledge jammed against the wall and we came to a complete stop. Matt screamed at the dogs and I pushed with all my might but it wouldn't budge—it was frozen in place.

"Rock the sledge!" Matt yelled. "Get it free!"

I tried to move the sledge over. It wouldn't move. It didn't budge. It had to weigh almost three times as much as me.

"Come on, Danny, shift it over! Put some muscle behind it!"

I grabbed one handle with both hands and braced my legs against the ice wall. I used my legs to push while I pulled with my hands. I felt the handle bending. Something was going to give and—the sledge popped over!

"Good work, Danny!"

We started moving forward and I let go of the handles. The sledge surged up the slope and I scrambled to catch up. Maybe for a while I could be pulled along instead of pushing. The dogs were digging in—they were glad to be free as well.

I thought about Captain Bartlett. It was hard enough to get a sledge through this gap, but he had actually carved this passage using nothing more than a pick and an axe. It was amazing—but nothing that I wouldn't have expected from the Captain. I knew he'd get the ship up here and I knew he'd find, or make, or break a trail that would take Peary to the Pole. Funny, everybody knew that Commander Peary was in command of this expedition, but I thought everybody also knew who the real leader was—the Captain.

The sledge suddenly tilted forward—we were going down—we'd passed the peak. I could see the end of the ridge and beyond that flat, clear ice. We were as good as through!

I KNEW THAT we couldn't move much farther that night. The sun was close to the horizon and was sinking fast. We had, at most, an hour of direct light and then perhaps another thirty minutes after the sun set when the light would still shine from beneath the horizon. We'd have to stop and make camp soon. Oatah and Matt could build us a shelter pretty fast. That was reassuring . . . and disturbing. I wanted to stop. I wanted to rest. I *needed* to sleep. I just didn't want to do that inside an igloo. If there was any chance I could have slept outside I would have, but the cold and wind made that impossible. I guess I had no choice but to sleep inside the igloo—or at least *try* to sleep. I didn't know if the fears in my heart would allow my eyes to close.

To make matters even worse, the ice was becoming less stable. We were following along the trail the Captain had marked, but three times we'd had to change our direction to get around open water or fresh leads . . . places that had been solid ice when the Captain had passed by not so long ago. We'd moved around those spots and then returned to the trail that the Captain had blazed. We were still on track, but those detours had delayed us. If not for those side trips we might have caught up to the Captain tonight, or tomorrow at worst, but that wasn't going to happen.

There was a rifle shot! I jerked my head up and scanned the horizon. A second shot! That could mean only one thing—it had to be the Captain and George!

I jumped up onto the runners and looked ahead. There up on the ice, not far ahead of us, were two sledges, two teams, and two men, waving their arms in the air. I didn't have Eskimo eyes to know for sure that it was the Captain and George, but who else could it be? I was grateful to see them, to catch up, but there was no way we *should* have caught them. They should have been farther along the trail. Why were they here? I didn't know the answers, but I knew we'd find out soon enough.

Matt had picked up the pace and Oatah and his team had matched his speed. Even Commander Peary was moving faster, although the other two sledges were pulling away. I probably couldn't have kept up with them, but I could at least have passed the Commander—but I knew better. Instead of running I stayed on the runners. Since I couldn't rush I might as well rest.

The two sledges pulled away, farther and farther as we all got closer. I could now make out the outline of two igloos. They had slept here and prepared another for the arrival of the next group. Why had they stopped instead of travelling farther? The ice looked clear and open and . . . there was something different about the ice . . . it was the wrong colour . . . No, it was the right colour . . . for open water. Stretched out for hundreds and hundreds of yards was open water, from one side of the horizon to the other. There wasn't any need to rush. I now knew why they'd stopped. They *couldn't* go any farther.

Chapter Twenty-Three

March 10, 1909

I SLID OUT through the tunnel, stood up, and brushed off the snow. That was the last box of supplies from the last load, all safely put away in the igloo. It was one of six igloos that had been constructed right here at the water's edge over the past five days. Three of them were now completely filled with supplies. Dr. Goodsell, Mr. Marvin, Mr. MacMillan, and a dozen different Eskimos had all brought out supplies, stayed the night, and then turned back around to get more. My job was to stay there, put those supplies away, and wait. Wait along with the Commander. We just stayed there, waiting for the ice to freeze over or drift together so we could cross.

Commander Peary was standing at the edge of the ice. He'd been standing there for the last hour, not moving, just staring out at the water—or more likely the ice on the other side of the water, or that imaginary point, the Pole, beyond that. It was as if he was trying to *will* the ice to come closer, commanding the water to freeze. He had spent a lot of time like that. Standing, staring, silent, not talking. And, other than the people dropping off supplies, we had been alone for the better part of two days. That was when the Captain and

George, tired of waiting for the ice to freeze, had gone off in one direction along the open water and Matt and Oatah had gone the other way. Since neither group had come back, I could only assume that neither had found a way around the open lead and that it had to go on for at least twenty miles in both directions.

Slowly I walked over to join the Commander. The wind was strong, coming directly from the north, straight into my face. I stopped a few steps back and waited. I didn't want to disturb him. A minute passed, and then another. I didn't want to bother him but I didn't want to wait forever, either. The wind was strong and cold and bitter. I cleared my throat and he turned around.

"The supplies are all stowed, sir."

"Good, boy. You must think I'm half crazy, standing here looking out over the water."

"No, sir," I said quickly, hoping he hadn't been reading my thoughts.

"It is very difficult," he said, "standing here, watching the dream of a lifetime vanish before my eyes. Do you know how painful that is, Danny?"

"No, sir . . . but I know it must be hard."

"Harder than you could even imagine. This is something that I have dreamed of for most of my adult life. Other times that I have failed I could always hold out faith that there would still be another time, another chance . . . but this time . . . " He let the sentence trail off. There was no need to finish.

"But all is not lost yet," he said after a while. "Do you feel that breeze?"

I nodded. It would have been hard to miss.

"The pans of ice are coming together. The gap is closing."

I looked out at the water. The gap was narrower than it had been at any time since we'd first arrived, but it was still at least fifty yards across.

"At the present rate, the way it is closing, the two pans of ice could come together in a matter of hours. And the instant it closes we move forward. You and me, Danny."

"Us?"

"If no one else is here we will strike out together. We can't wait and risk the gap opening again."

"But . . . but . . . what if it opens again after we pass?"

"If it closed once it will close again and the Captain will follow us, assuming he hasn't already found a way around it. We need to get two sledges loaded with enough supplies for two men and twenty dogs, to last for as many days as we can load. You'd better get the sledges ready."

I couldn't believe my ears. Why hadn't he told me this two hours ago before I unloaded the two sledges that had been left? I almost said something. Instead I spun around on my heel to follow orders. I walked away, muttering under my breath. Wasn't he going to at least help me? He was the Commander and all, but if he really wanted them loaded fast he could help load . . .

I heard a scream and a crash.

I spun around. Where was the Commander? He was gone! No, there he was—his arms and head were above the water—he'd crashed through the ice! For a split second, I froze in place, unable to understand what I was seeing, or what I should do. Then I came to and I started running toward him and—

"Get back, Danny!" he yelled. "Don't come any closer!"

I skidded to a stop.

"The ice won't hold you!" he called out. "Get a rope . . . get something to pull me out!"

I ran back for the rope that was on my sledge. Every sledge had rope as part of its survival pack. I threw off the canvas . . . where was the rope? I grabbed a canvas bag and tossed it out of the way. The rope was underneath. I took the rope and ran back toward Commander Peary.

He was in the water, his arms on the ice, scrambling, clawing, grabbing, trying to get a finger hold to pull himself up. The ice kept breaking and crumbling beneath his weight. There was nothing he could do to pull himself out. The weight of his clothing was pulling him down even as he tried to lift himself up. I ran as close as I could get, and then, holding onto one end of the rope, I tossed it to him!

The wind caught the rope and blew it back toward me, causing it to land well short of his reach. I pulled it back in and threw it again. It missed by even more. I had to get closer. I took one step and then another and my foot crashed through the ice! I stumbled, crashing forward, landing with a thud—but thank goodness *on* the ice, not *through* the ice! I started to pull myself up and then remembered what I'd been told. I stayed on my belly to distribute my weight evenly and scrambled like a crab, away from the opening. I retreated to solid ice—

what I hoped was solid ice—and hesitantly got to my knees. It held. I stood up.

"Hurry, Danny, hurry!"

I needed to hurry, but hurry and do what? I had to think. I had to get closer to get the rope to him, but how could I get closer without falling through? I had an idea.

I ran back to the dogs. I grabbed Lightning's lead and ripped it from the stake holding him in place. I took the rope and tried to tie it to his lead. My fingers didn't want to work right. The rope was thick and stiff and my hands were numb. I fumbled around, threading the rope through, tightening it. It had to be tight, the knot had to hold. It had to.

"Come on, boy!" I yelled and Lightning ran with me back toward the open water.

"I'm coming, Commander!" I called out.

"Down!" I yelled, and Lightning sank to the ice.

I took a few more steps and could feel the ice sinking and crunching under my feet. I stopped and fell to my knees. I wrapped the rope around my wrist and then, on my belly, head first, I scurried forward. From my viewpoint, just barely above the ice, I could see the Commander's head and shoulders and arms, clinging to the ice, but I couldn't see the open water. I was grateful I couldn't see the water.

"Careful, Danny, careful," he said as I closed in. His voice was shaky and soft. I knew the ice was sucking away his warmth and his life with it. He couldn't hold on much longer. I moved as close as I could. I needed to hand him the rope. Maybe I even needed to tie the rope onto his arm. Just a few more feet . . . a few more inches and I'd be able to—I crashed through the ice and my whole body slipped into the freezing-cold water!

It felt as if my whole body had been slapped, shocked by the explosion of cold against my skin! I struggled to get my head above water, clawing my way up, and broke the surface! I tried to gain a grip against the ice but I couldn't! I pulled at the rope, pulling in the slack until it became taut. Lightning stayed down, anchoring the other end. I pulled up, hand over hand, slowly moving myself out of the water and onto the ice, inch by inch, until I was finally out!

I was completely out of breath and gasped for air. I was out, but I needed to get farther away to solid ice so I didn't fall through again and . . . I couldn't. The Commander was still in the water. I needed to get him out. I untied the rope from my wrist and carefully slid toward him, thinking that the ice was going to give under me again. I was so close. I could see the Commander, see his eyes, still bright, pleading with me to help, his outstretched hand just a few inches away. I reached forward, straining to get those inches. He grabbed the rope!

"Tie it around you," I said.

I spun around on my belly and scuttled away, sliding toward Lightning. He stayed down on the ice. I got to my knees and tried to rise to my feet but stumbled over. My clothes were heavy and wet and they were starting to freeze solid. I got back to my feet.

"Up!" I yelled, and Lightning jumped up.

I grabbed his lead and started to pull him away. The slack in the rope got played out and then we staggered to a stop. All the slack was gone. Now we had to work.

"Is the rope tied on?" I screamed.

"Yes." His voice was faint. He was fading, the cold was taking him.

"Pull!" I screamed at Lightning, and at the same time I grabbed the lead and pulled as hard as I could. Lightning's claws dug into the ice, scratching forward, pulling and pulling. We were hardly moving . . . a few inches . . . a few feet. I turned around. He was out of the water!

"Pull! Pull!" I called and the two of us hauled him farther away from the water, dragging him across the ice. It was much easier to move him now. He was well clear of the open lead.

"Sit!" I said, and Lightning dropped down.

I stumbled back down along the rope to where the Commander lay on the ice. He was out of the water, but he wasn't moving!

"Commander! Commander!"

He lifted up his head and tried to rise, pushing himself up on one arm. His arm collapsed and he slumped back down. I grabbed him.

"You have to get up!"

"I need . . . I need to get my breath," he gasped. "I need to rest."

"You need to get up!" I screamed. I knew that lying there was the worst thing he could do.

I pulled him up and he struggled to rise. He leaned against me. He was heavy, and for an instant I thought we were both going to topple over. He stood up straight. His arm was around my shoulders, but at least we were up.

"We have to get to the igloo. We have to get dry clothing," I said.

With the Commander leaning heavily against me we moved, slowly, across the ice. The igloo wasn't far. We were going to make it. We were going to live!

I SIPPED the warm, strong coffee that the Commander had made after we had both changed into dry clothing. He had a blanket around his shoulders as well. He'd been in the water a lot longer than me and was still shaking. We hadn't exchanged many words. We just sat there, drinking our coffee. It was good coffee. It felt good going down and formed a hot pocket in the middle of my stomach, from which little feelers of warmth were starting to spread.

"More?" Commander Peary asked as he held out the pot.

"Yes . . . please . . . sir," I said, offering my cup.

As he filled it I noticed that his hand was shaking badly.

"Thanks."

"It should be me thanking you," Commander Peary said. "First you save my daughter's life, and now you save her father's. I would have died out there without your help."

I didn't know what to say. I just stared down at my coffee.

"I thought I *was* going to die," he said. He took a sip of his coffee. "I just thought about letting go . . . slipping under the water . . . giving in to the cold."

That was the last thing I had ever expected him to say.

"And the thought that I was going to die wasn't frightening. It was peaceful, almost reassuring." He looked up at me. "I thought about how the Pole was slipping out of my grasp and how death was a welcome alternative. I would have died a hero rather than lived as a failure."

We sat there in silence, sipping our coffee, letting his words sink in.

"Have you ever felt like giving up?" Commander Peary asked.

"When my mother died," I said, without even needing to think. I'd never said that to anybody before.

"That must have been an awful time. But you didn't . . . you didn't give up."

"I wanted to, but I didn't."

"Do you know the difference between failure and success?" Commander Peary asked.

I shook my head.

"Success is simply failure that refused to give up. And that is why, after failing before and again, I will now reach the Pole. I will be remembered not as a failure, not as a hero who perished in the effort, but as the conqueror of the Pole . . . Peary of the Pole."

"I always knew you were going to make it to the Pole," I said.

"Even when I was in the water?"

"Yes, sir. No doubt."

"You are a true blessing, Danny." He paused. "I would consider it a great favour if you did not repeat this conversation," Commander Peary said.

"I won't, sir. I won't tell anybody anything about what happened."

"That might be wise. It would not be good for the morale of the men. They need to see me as a tower of confidence."

"That is how they do see you, sir."

He placed a hand on my shoulder. "Then let us keep it that way."

Chapter Twenty-Four

April 1, 1909

THE DOGS had all been fed. I circled around the sledge so that it was between me and the wind and slumped down to the ice. I pulled a piece of jerky out of my pocket and chomped down on it. There was no taste to it. That didn't surprise me. Nothing tasted good, or bad, or anything. It was no longer food. It was just fuel. It was just like throwing another log on a fire to keep it burning. That was the reason we ate, to keep the fire burning inside of us, to fuel us to keep moving forward. I thought back to when the pemmican tasted bad. And then it tasted good. Now it tasted like nothing.

It had been twenty-five days . . . or was it twenty-six days since we'd left the camp? It could have been either, or maybe twenty-seven or twenty-eight. I'd stopped trying to keep track. It all just blurred together. Day after day, hour after hour, moving across the frozen waste. Mostly it was just an endless stream of movement across a world without colour or warmth or end, broken up by fitful disturbed sleep and the occasional burst of panic. Somebody falling through the ice, a close brush with a polar bear, dogs breaking free in the night and needing to be caught.

Since the Big Lead, since the Commander and I had gone through the ice, I had been with him and Matt. The Captain kept breaking trail along with George and Oatah and sometimes Seegloo and Ookeah. Mr. Marvin, Dr. Goodsell, and Mr. MacMillan sometimes were with us, sometimes in front, and sometimes behind, bringing up supplies. And, of course, there was also a steady stream of Eskimos bringing provisions forward, re-supplying us with what we needed to keep surging toward the Pole.

"Mind if I join you?" It was George.

We had caught up with George and his group yesterday, and there had been so many small ridges for them to cut through that they hadn't been able to pull away from us again. He sat down beside me.

"Did you ever think you'd get this close to the Pole?" he asked.

"How close are we?"

"Captain Bartlett's last reading placed us at eighty-seven degrees and twenty-four minutes north. That would mean we are just over one hundred and seventy miles from the Pole."

"How many people 'ave ever been this far north?" I asked.

"How many people are in our party?"

"You mean . . . ?"

He smiled. "This is it, this is the record. The farthest north ever reached. Of course, that record will only hold until we start moving again. We are as close to sitting on the top of the world as anyone has ever been."

"How many days' travel to the Pole?"

"Captain Bartlett would be a better person to ask. Much depends on the ice conditions, the weather, ridges, any open water we might encounter, and how they are planning to push at the end."

"Push?"

"They'll lighten the load for the sprint to the Pole so they can run faster and harder . . . maybe seven days. The only question is, who will Commander Peary take with him?"

"Do you think he'll take you?"

George shook his head. "I wish I knew. I was pleased when he let me stay and sent back the other members of the expedition."

Mr. Marvin, Mr. MacMillan, and Dr. Goodsell had joined us two days before with additional supplies. That was when the Commander had told them: they were leaving their supplies and heading back. They weren't coming any farther. Of course, I wasn't there when he told them, but I had seen them just after. They were disappointed, but understood that it was the Commander's decision to make. When they left the next morning they wished us well.

"Has he said anything to you?" George asked.

"Me? Why do you think he would 'ave told me?" I asked.

"You and the Commander are pretty close, especially since that time at the Big Lead. Did something happen back there?"

"What do you mean?" I asked, trying to sound innocent. "We just sat around an' waited." I didn't like lying to George, but I had kept my word. Nobody knew, and nobody was going to know. Not just about what we had talked about, but that the Commander had fallen through the ice.

"Who do you think he'll bring along?" I asked.

"Matt, of course, Captain Bartlett to break trail, and at least two of the Eskimos."

"Not us?"

"I'd like to go. To come this far without finishing would be painful, but I have to be realistic and accept whatever he says. I think you and I are on borrowed time right now. It won't be long before he orders us to turn back, so enjoy it while you can."

Enjoy it . . . what a strange way of putting it. Bone-chilling cold, fitful sleep, bad food, constant danger of losing our lives, being pushed to the brink of physical exhaustion. *Enjoy* wasn't the right word, but I did know I was glad to be there and would be sad when I was told that my time was over, that I'd have to turn around. Then again . . . I couldn't help but wonder.

"The Captain's leaving again," George said as he practically jumped to his feet.

Captain Bartlett, followed by Oatah and his team, was off. Their sledges were practically empty. Since they were breaking trail they had only the basics with them—markers to show us the way, picks and axes to cut through ridges, extra clothing in case they fell through a fresh lead, and rifles.

I knew that George was going to try to follow them immediately but that I didn't have to leave yet. I could rest, wait until the Commander signalled that it was time for us to go, but I wanted to be ready when that time came.

I put a hand against the sledge and pulled myself up. I walked along my team, pulling at the leads, checking to make sure the knots were all tight. Lightning was already up and tugging slightly at the lines. We watched as George and Seegloo and Ookeah started off, and I knew Lightning wanted to join them. All three had heavily loaded sledges and they would be moving more slowly than the Captain would be. That left the Commander, Matt, and me. In some ways it didn't seem fair that we got to travel a path that was already broken, but that was deliberate. The final assault would be done in a terrible rush, with almost no sleep and hardly any time to eat, and the Commander and Matt had to be saved for that . . . But what about the Captain? Maybe somebody else should have been breaking trail to save *him* . . . but who else could do it? Then again, knowing the Captain the way I did, maybe he didn't need any rest.

I undid the top two clasps of my parka. The temperature certainly wasn't what anybody would have described as warm, but it was warmer than it had been. The sun was almost always up there in the sky. We had almost sixteen hours of direct sun and another two or three hours when it was still light enough to move. And, with all that light, we were travelling longer each day. I didn't know the distances exactly. Some days we went farther than others. That had little to do with the time and more to do with the conditions of the ice.

I still thought about the ice, but I wasn't worried about it any more. I hadn't worried much since we'd left the Big Lead. Funny, but falling through the ice hadn't been a worry to me since I *had* fallen through. It had been a bad experience, certainly one I didn't want to repeat, but I had done it and survived. And if it happened again I'd survive again. Now my main concern about open water and fresh leads and pressure ridges was that they slowed us down. I knew we didn't have that much time left. The season was changing. We had only so long—that window, as Captain Bartlett called it—before the ocean ice would become so unstable that we could-n't travel on it safely. Hopefully that wouldn't happen before we reached the Pole. Hopefully it wouldn't happen before we finished reaching the Pole and were back on land.

WE WERE COMING UP to the next camp. The sledges were lined up, the dogs pinned down to the ice, and two little igloos already constructed. The sun was just setting, so our timing was perfect. We glided into the camp. It would be good to stop, eat, rest, and get a few hours of sleep.

"Danny," Commander Peary said. "Care for all of our dogs."

"Yes, sir."

Of course I'd do what I was ordered, but I wondered why. Usually Matt insisted on taking care of his dogs himself. I tended to the dogs but kept one eye on the Commander and Matt. They walked away from the igloos. They squatted down, their backs to the camp, and talked. I couldn't *know* what they were talking about, but I had an idea. Ever since my talk with George earlier in the day I'd thought about when they were going to make the decision to send back the last party, to start the all-out final assault. I had been thinking that it might be now. If I was right, I'd know soon enough. They stood up and walked back toward the camp.

"The Commander wants to talk to everybody," Matt said as he came over to me.

"What does he want to talk about?"

"You'll find out soon enough."

"Should I finish with the dogs, first?" I asked.

"Take a few minutes. The dogs always have to be cared for first."

Matt walked away to speak to George and then George walked over to me.

"Well?" he asked. "Do you think this is the end for us?"

I nodded my head. "That's what I was thinking. I guess we'll find out as soon as I finish with the dogs."

"And Captain Bartlett returns."

"Returns? Where is he?"

"While we were building the igloos and setting up camp he kept moving north, marking the first few miles of the trail for tomorrow."

I laughed. "I guess I shouldn't be surprised."

"Captain Bob is the most determined, dedicated man I have ever had the honour of knowing. I don't know where this expedition would have been if not for him. He has almost single-handedly marked and broken trail the entire time. He is one stubborn Newfoundlander . . . or is that saying the same thing twice?"

I laughed. "My mother would'a said that it was."

"Now, let me help you with the dogs and we'll catch some grub before the Captain returns."

WE STOOD IN A CIRCLE with the Commander in the centre. He had been talking for almost five minutes but he hadn't actually said anything yet, and the longer he talked the more certain I was that I knew what he was eventually going to say.

"I want to say how proud I am of all of you. As we stand here, at almost the eighty-eighth degree of latitude, we are farther north than any man has ever reached."

I thought that wasn't quite right. Captain Bartlett had been two miles farther north than any of the rest of us before he came back to camp.

"You need to remember this moment forever. Savour your accomplishment and remember that this would not be possible for any of us if not for all of us. We have been a team."

He stopped talking. I guessed he really did want us to savour the moment. I looked beyond the circle, beyond the igloos and sledges and dogs pegged down to the ice. I looked north, trying to picture that spot, less than one hundred and forty miles north, that spot I would only ever see in my mind. I felt a terrible sense of loss. To come this far was an incredible story of success. To come this far and have to leave was just as much a mark of failure.

"It is now my duty to inform you of my final decision. We cannot all make the final assault. Some must return," Commander Peary said.

He turned to face George. "I must inform you, dear sir, that you will be heading south."

"Yes, sir, I understand, sir. It has been my honour to have served you and to have come this far."

"You have been both faithful and strong and I offer you my sincere thanks."

They shook hands.

He turned to me. "Danny."

For a split second I thought I was about to start crying.

"You have come farther than any of us would ever have imagined or believed possible. It is as Captain Bartlett said: you are not a boy, but a man, who has proven his worth at every step of the way. You will be returning with George."

I felt disappointed and relieved. It had been harder waiting to hear than actually hearing. We shook hands. I guess I should have said something noble, but I was working hard to not show my emotions.

"Ookeah, Egingwah, and Kirik, you three will be returning south as well," Commander Peary said.

Kirik and Egingwah smiled. Ookeah gave a slight nod of his head to acknowledge he had heard and agreed. He didn't look pleased or displeased. He probably didn't care.

"You have been faithful servants and will be given additional gifts of iron knives and an extra large cooking pot for your efforts."

Now all three looked happy.

"And leading the returning team," Commander Peary said, "will be Captain Bartlett."

My eyes widened in surprise and I almost gasped out loud. I looked at the Captain. I tried to read his reaction but his face was a mask. I turned to George. He looked as shocked as I felt.

"Without you, Captain, this expedition would have floundered on the ocean before it even began. Now I need your expertise and determination to provide me with a safe route of retreat. For without that route I shall reach the Pole and then perish upon the return."

"I will not fail you, Commander," the Captain said.

"Of that I have no doubt. In the morn, six sledges will start south, each with a team of five dogs."

"You want half of my team?" I said out loud without even thinking. I was prepared to return south but not to give up Lightning or Blackie.

"Your lead dog will stay with you, Danny," Commander Peary said.

"Thanks, I mean, he's yours if you want him, sir."

"A generous offer, but I would not separate you from that dog. He will return leading your smaller team."

"Could Blackie come as well?" I asked.

"You choose your dogs, Danny," he said. "The four remaining sledges, piloted by myself, Matthew, Oatah, and Seegloo, will begin the final assault. Now, let us prepare our last meal together and repair to the igloos for a final sleep before the long day ahead."

I QUIETLY CAME UP to the Captain from behind. He hadn't heard me yet. He had been standing there by himself on the outskirts of the camp for so long that I'd had time to think about going to speak to him and then talked myself out of it three times and started into a fourth. I'd even walked partway out once before turning tail and retreating back to the igloos. This time I wasn't going back. I was armed with an excuse to be there.

"I brought you a cup of coffee, Cap'n."

He turned around. "Thanks, Danny." He took the cup and had a sip.

"I made it special the way ya like it, sir, with four heaping spoons of sugar."

"That is the way I like it, although even the sweetness of this coffee cannot overcome the bitter taste in my mouth."

"Do ya want me to get more sugar, sir?"

He laughed. "Not enough sugar in the entire tropics to take away that taste, I'm afraid."

I wasn't sure what to say next, but I knew what I wanted to say. "I was sort of surprised when he chose not to have ya come with him."

"As was I," he said softly. "And disappointed. I thought I had been given both the promise and 'ad also earned the privilege of the Pole."

"We all know what you did, Cap'n. All of us."

"Thank you for sayin' that, Danny. Now, there is no point in cryin' over spilled milk. Sometimes things just aren't fair . . . but who said life was fair? Sometimes there's nothing fair about it. You know, Danny, I really admire you."

"Me?" I asked in shock.

"You. Your life had some turns and spills that no young lad should have to endure."

Of course I knew what he was talking about—the death of my parents.

"But somehow you found a way to go on."

"To be honest with ya, sir," I told him, "I didn't see as I really had much choice about it." And that was how

I felt, that most of what I'd been doing since my mother died was just putting one foot in front of the other and, lately, hoping I didn't fall through the ice to what was waiting below.

"That's what I mean," the Captain said. "And do you know why ya didn't quit?"

I shook my head.

"Let me tell you a story."

"A story?"

"Maybe it's more like a joke," he said. "There's these two sailors, two good lads from St. John's, an' they've been sailin' together for the better part of twenty years. One of them finishes his shift and is hurryin' off to play some dice. His friend grabs 'im by the arm and says, 'You don't want to be playin' in that game 'cause those dice is fixed . . . ya can't win.' His friend says he knows the game is fixed and he's gonna lose, 'But buddy, I know the game ain't fair and I'm gonna lose,' he says, 'but it's the only game on the ship.'" He looked at me but didn't say a word. Finally he spoke.

"I'm gonna accept what the Commander said. Just like you accepted what 'appened to your parents. We go on, because it's the only game we 'ave to play. We have no choice but to go on. Fair or not fair, it's what we have to do. Understand?"

I nodded my head.

"You're no quitter. You took the worst things that could 'appen to a lad and became somebody I'm proud to know, somebody I respect an' look up to."

"You respect me?"

"Don't sound so surprised. Now, let's not waste any more breath on talkin' about things. What's done is done and there's nothing that nobody can do to change that."

He was right. It was over and there was nothing that could be done . . . or was there?

I CRAWLED THROUGH the entrance to the igloo—the igloo of the Commander and Matt. I could see light around the skins hung over the entrance to block out the wind and cold. The light meant they were still awake. I poked my head through the curtain. Matt was reading the Bible and the Commander was writing in his journal.

"Permission to speak to you, sir?" I asked.

"You need no permission. Please."

I crawled the rest of the way in and stood up. "Could we speak privately?"

I could tell that my question had caught them by surprise.

"I'll leave you two gentlemen alone," Matt responded immediately. He put his Bible down on his skin bed and crawled out through the opening.

"This must be important," Commander Peary said.

"Yes, sir." Now that I was there and had permission to speak I felt hesitant.

"Don't be shy, Danny. We've been through too much together for that."

"Yes, sir." I gathered my words. "Before on the ship . . . with your daughter . . . "

"When you saved her life."

I nodded. "You said you owed me a debt."

"Yes, I both said and meant that. I owe you a debt so enormous it is almost beyond words. Have you come here to claim that debt?"

I nodded my head ever so slightly.

"Although I do not feel it is wise, I feel that I have no choice but to honour that debt. I will allow you to accompany me to the Pole."

"Me?" I gasped.

"Yes, you will be coming with me."

"But . . . but . . . you don't understand. I didn't come 'ere to ask you to take me!"

"You didn't?" He was obviously surprised, confused.

"No, sir. I was going to ask if you would take the Cap'n with you."

Now he looked shocked. He quickly recovered. "Does the Captain know that you are speaking to me about this request?"

"No, sir."

"That is wise."

I wasn't sure why that was wise but I nodded in agreement.

"I owe a great debt," he said, "but I owe that debt to *you,* not to Captain Bartlett."

"But he's done so much to get you this far," I argued.

"No doubt. Without him, this mission would not have succeeded. He has performed these tasks admirably, outstandingly. But, he has simply been fulfilling his orders as a member of this expedition under my command. Now it is time for him to follow different orders. I need the Captain to secure the return route. There may be new ridges that have formed, there will be more open water and routes that need to be scouted." He paused. "Let me ask you a question: who would you trust more to mark that route than Captain Bartlett?"

I didn't even need to think. "Nobody."

"Indeed. And that return route is the very lifeline of the members of the final party. Does that party include you?"

"You mean I can still come with you?"

"My offer was made and it stands. Are you in?"

My instant response was to say no. I didn't know if it was out of fear or the sense that it was unfair that I should go and the Captain couldn't. But I did want to come.

"I'm in."

Chapter Twenty-Five

April 2, 1909

I CRAWLED THROUGH the entrance. The cold air of outside met me halfway. The sun was still below the horizon so that meant it was somewhere before three in the morning. The sun was now in the sky almost all the time. It would disappear briefly beneath the horizon for a couple of hours, but even then it didn't get dark, as the light reflected up over the horizon. There was still enough light for me to see that at least half the party was already awake and up. That didn't surprise me. I could sense the excitement in the air the night before.

Matt and George and Oatah were standing together and I joined them.

"Danny, I saw you speak to the Captain last night. Did he say anything to you?" Matt asked.

"Say anything? . . . I don't know what you mean."

"Did he say anything about leaving?"

"I don't understand."

"He's gone," George said.

"Gone! He can't be gone! Have you checked in the igloos? He must still be sleeping or—"

"His sledge is gone. His team is gone," Matt said.

"He headed north," George said.

"How do you know that if you didn't see him leave?" I questioned.

"Tracks." Oatah pointed at the ice. "Leaving for north. Old."

"Oatah thinks he left sometime in the middle of the night. Did he say anything to you at all, Danny, anything that would help us?" Matt asked.

"He just said he was disappointed, but that he would do what he was ordered to do. That's all."

If he had headed north—and I knew that what Oatah was saying had to be true—then he wasn't following orders. But what was he doing? He couldn't have been heading for the Pole by himself . . . could he?

"Somebody has to inform the Commander," George said.

"He doesn't know?"

"Not yet," Matt said. "I think that task falls to me."

He turned to leave and I grabbed him by the sleeve. "No, you don't have to tell the Commander anything . . . he's back."

The sun had continued to rise. I could now see a small black smudge to the north. It had to be the Captain silhouetted against the sun. We stood there in silence, watching, as the sun rose, warming our faces as it continued to rise and the Captain continued to come closer. As he closed in all the dogs in the camp began yelping and barking and howling to welcome back the team. He brought his sledge to a stop just steps away from us.

"Oatah, can you tend to the dogs?" the Captain said. "And choose the five best suited to join your team."

"We didn't know where you were," George said.

"I was out on the trail."

"But you came from the north," George said.

"I've broken and marked the first nine miles of the trail . . . could have got farther but I had to cut through a number of pressure ridges . . . one was fierce big."

"But how is that possible?" George asked. "How could you travel that far?"

"First mile or so I did yesterday when the igloos were being prepared. The last seven I did in the middle of the night."

"Did you sleep at all?" George asked.

"There will be plenty of time for sleep when we get back to land. At the last marker you'll find a cache of supplies under a canvas—not much of anything but enough food to feed some of the dogs. I also took a reading. That spot is eighty-eight degrees and forty-eight minutes north. That is just over ninety miles from the Pole. Until you pass that spot, for a few brief hours, I lay claim to 'avin' travelled the farthest north of any man."

"My hearty congratulations on your accomplishment!" George said. The two men took off their mitts and shook hands.

"I just wish I could be there to offer my congratulations when that mark is surpassed," Captain Bartlett said.

"You should be there," George said. "You should be there when the Pole is reached."

"That is not my destiny."

"But I'm saying it *should* be!" George said. "I understand me being sent back, but not you. Without your gallant efforts no man would reach the Pole! It is not fair that—"

"Enough!" Captain Bartlett said forcefully, cutting George off cold. "It's not your place or mine to question the orders of the Commander of this expedition, just as I would expect you to follow my orders if we were aboard the *Roosevelt*."

"I was just saying—"

"I appreciate your words, George," he said, "but this is the last I want to hear of it. Our orders are to be followed, without question. Understood?"

He hesitated. "Yes . . . I know you are right. Sorry for the breach of etiquette. I hope my lack of judgment will not be repeated to the Commander."

We all looked at Matt. "Nothing said here will be repeated, especially in light of the fact that I agree with your statements. Be honest, Bob, you must have felt some anger at not being included."

"Anger is not the right word. Disappointment, yes. Sadness. I even shed a tear or two, but that's all."

"What you did last night, this final gift of nine miles of trail, is the mark of a true gentleman. And more important, a true friend," Matt said.

"A friend I am, but I was just listenin' to the words of our Saviour, 'Do unto others as you would have them do unto you.'" He paused. "Now we must all prepare for our parting." He turned to me. "Danny, have you decided which dogs you will leave behind?"

Of course he didn't know I wasn't leaving because he'd been gone. I felt uneasy.

"Danny won't be returning to the camp," Matt said. "The Commander has decided he will accompany us to the Pole."

"What?" Captain Bartlett asked, sounding and looking shocked.

"Danny is the fifth member of our assault on the Pole," Matt repeated.

The Captain's eyes burned and he opened his mouth to say something, but he didn't. He took a deep breath before he continued. "It is the right of the Commander to make such decisions." He stepped forward and shook my hand. "Well deserved and fittin' that a Newfoundlander should put 'is boot on the Pole."

"Thanks, sir." He wasn't mad. He was happy for me.

Captain Bartlett turned directly to Matt. "My dear friend, I now need to ask a favour of you."

"Anything, Bob, you know that."

"Danny here is under the command of Commander Peary, but he is to be your responsibility. It is your duty to return him, safe, to the *Roosevelt*."

"You have my word, Captain. Danny will be by my side regardless of the outcome."

"I will hold you to that word, Matthew. We will ultimately meet in one of three places . . . Heaven, Hell, or the *Roosevelt*."

Chapter Twenty-Six

April 5, 1909

"DANNY, WAKE UP!" It was Matt. He was standing over me and gently shaking my arm.

I started and tried to jump to my feet, but he held me in place.

"It's okay," he said reassuringly.

"I didn't mean to fall asleep," I apologized.

"You needed to sleep."

It was then that I noticed that I had a skin over top of me as a blanket.

"How long did I sleep?"

"Almost an hour. It's time to get moving again."

I threw off the skin that was covering me and put my hand against the sledge to steady me as I rose to my feet. I picked up the second skin that had been my bed, the thin shield between me and the ice underneath. I tried to fold up the skins and tuck them back onto my sledge, but my fingers were numb and aching.

"What time is it?" I asked.

Matt shook his head. "Nine . . . ten . . . maybe midnight . . . I'm not sure. Does it matter?"

I shook my head. It didn't, and I was almost too tired to care. The hours all blurred together. It was like I'd imagine a desert would be like—except for the cold. A few short months ago I could only dream of sunlight as we endured constant darkness. Now I just wanted it to set and stay down long enough for us to sleep, to rest, to escape its constantly staring down on us. Not only wasn't I sure what time it was, I wasn't sure of the date, or the number of days that had passed since we'd started the final assault. It was two days . . . no three . . . it couldn't be four . . . not yet anyway . . . or was it?

Instinctively I walked alongside my team. The dogs hadn't even been taken off their leads. They had just rested, in harness, ready to move. Fifteen dogs, with Lightning still the faithful leader that I needed. Even Lightning looked tired, though. We had been in almost constant motion. Four or five hours of straight sledging, followed by a few minutes of rest, some food, and then a chance to sleep for a few hours every third march. It was no wonder I didn't know the time or day. It was all blurring together. It had a dreamlike quality. No, a *nightmare* quality. Why had I asked to come along? I just wanted to be home. Not at the base camp. Not on the *Roosevelt*. Home in my bed in my house and . . . wait, I didn't have a house . . . I didn't have a home. Maybe at my sister's house. Was *that* my home? Was any place ever going to be home for me again?

"You ready to go?" Matt asked.

"Sure . . . yeah . . . wait . . . where is everybody else?" Matt and I and our teams were the only ones there.

"Oatah and Seegloo are breaking trail and the Commander is following behind them. You just fell asleep and the Commander said we should leave you to sleep for a while."

"You should have woken me up!"

"We thought it was better. We're all pretty close to the edge. I needed the rest as well."

"You?"

"This is pushing us all close to the brink. Besides, we'll catch them soon enough. Then you and I will take the lead and break trail."

"How much longer?"

"Depending on the ice conditions it might only take us an hour or two to catch up to the rest of our party."

"No," I said, "you don't understand. How much longer until we reach the Pole? How much farther do we still have to go?"

"The Commander last took a reading earlier today and we have travelled at least ten miles since then . . . so . . . no more than fifteen miles."

Fifteen. I wasn't sure if I should be happy or heartbroken. Fifteen miles seemed like it was so close, but yet so far. It was two marches . . . maybe three.

Matt ordered his team to their feet and my dogs instinctively followed his orders. It was time to go, whether I wanted to or not. There was no way to travel south until we had finished travelling north. There was no choice.

WE HAD EATEN some jerky and pemmican, slept, perched against our sledges and sandwiched between skins, for two hours before we had started once again. The sun traced an oval path circling the horizon.

The ice was remarkably smooth. The only ridges we'd encountered were small and we'd easily battered through them. Twice we'd come across fresh leads but even those were so small that our route only jogged over slightly to the side. The dogs were tired—we were all tired—but the sledges were almost empty. We'd been caching supplies along the way, supplies we'd use as we returned. Fifteen dogs, even fifteen tired dogs, could pull pretty fast.

As concerned as I was about us, the dogs were an even greater worry. Underneath their layers of thick fur they were starting to look thin and stretched out. A couple of dogs had come up lame—thank goodness not on my team—and had had to be killed. I'd heard the shots but hadn't seen them fall. I was worried about Lightning. He was still the leader, but even he seemed to have lost his passion. He looked almost as tired and worn out as I felt. I wanted to jump up on the runners and let the dogs pull me along, but I fought that urge. I knew if I was running alongside that the dogs would be better able to go on.

I felt sorry for Commander Peary's team. While there were virtually no supplies on his sledge, they still had to pull him along. He was a big man and he was riding the whole way now. He couldn't run beside. He didn't even seem to be able to push to help, and they had to be suffering under his weight.

Aside from the good ice conditions that were allowing us to move quickly, his riding on the sledge was the reason they hadn't caught up to us yet. If the Commander hadn't been along, if Captain Bartlett had taken his place, we could have been at the Pole and on our way back by now. I was exhausted, and it was hard not to feel angry at him for slowing us down. I tried to put those thoughts aside—I should have been grateful for all that he'd done for me, for his kindness, for allowing me to come to the Pole. I knew it was small and petty, but still, I had those feelings.

Up ahead Matt had brought his team to a stop. That could mean either there was a pressure ridge that needed to be hacked through or we were stopping for a bite. Either way, good or bad, I just wanted to stop. By the time I reached him it was obvious which. He had taken out the small stove and was melting snow. A hot cup of coffee would be welcome.

The second I ordered my team to halt the dogs dropped to the ice as one, exhausted. I was starting to worry more about two of the dogs in particular. They had seemed listless at our last stop and one of them hadn't even eaten all the blubber he had been given. That wasn't a good sign.

"We'll be waiting here until the others join us," Matt said.

"But we could go farther," I said. I had trouble believing I had just said that.

"We'll stay here. The position of the sun in the sky and the speed of our march might mean we don't have to go any farther."

"What do you . . . ?" I let the sentence trail off. Of course, I *knew* what he meant. "Are we here? Is this the Pole?"

"Only the Commander can tell. Only he can take a reading," Matt said. "Technically, the Pole is an area almost a mile wide. And until he takes a reading there is no point in travelling farther. Don't you want to rest?"

"I want to lie down and not get up for a month."

"A month you don't have. Two hours you do. Tend to the dogs, eat, and then lay your head down and sleep if you can, because you're going to need it."

"But you said we might be at the Pole so I might not have to go any farther."

"Even if this is the Pole, that only means you're *halfway* through your journey. We still have to get back to land."

My heart sank. Of course I knew what he was saying was right. It wasn't that I didn't know that. It was just different hearing the words. Somehow, being so focused on the goal of reaching the Pole, I had put away the part that followed.

"Hopefully we'll be moving along a completely marked trail, but there's no telling where that trail might lead," Matt said. "There's a greater chance of open water, or fresh leads. And even if Captain Bob marked a perfect trail, there's no telling what might happen in the days between his marking it and us reaching it. We've made it halfway, but perhaps the more difficult half is still to come."

I couldn't bear to believe that.

"Now go to sleep, rest, close your eyes."

I could lie down and I could close my eyes, but I didn't know if I could sleep any more.

THE DOGS might have been tired but not so tired that they didn't raise a commotion to tell us of the approach of the rest of the party. I had tried to sleep for the past two hours but I'd only been able to close my eyes for a few seconds before I'd been jarred awake. I felt too tired to get to sleep. My body was exhausted but my mind was racing. Excitement and fear were stronger than the exhaustion. Was it possible, were we really here? And if we were, could we get back? I almost didn't want to dream it was possible. Would that dream turn into a nightmare ? What would happen if the Big Lead had opened up again? How would we get past it? Would it close up again, or would the remaining ice simply melt underneath our feet?

As the sledges approached I heard the Commander's voice above the commotion of the dogs. I couldn't make out the words but he sounded angry. Matt came to the sledge as it stopped and the two men began talking. No, not talking—the Commander spoke with a raised voice and Matt listened. I still couldn't make out the words, though. Finally the Commander undid the canvas on his sledge and Matt walked away, toward where I stood.

"What's wrong?" I asked. I was afraid that we'd somehow gone off course or something bad had happened or—

"He was displeased because we've gone too far," Matt said.

"You mean we passed the Pole?"

Matt shook his head. "No. Because we *reached* the Pole."

"We're here . . . we're at the Pole?" I gasped.

"We'll know soon enough." Matt gestured to where the Commander stood. He was holding the sextant in his hands and lining it up with the sun. By knowing the time—he had a fancy watch—and the position of the sun he could tell our exact latitude.

"But why would he be mad if we are at the Pole?" I asked. "Shouldn't he be happy . . . isn't this his dream?"

"His dream is to be the *first* person to reach the Pole, not the third."

That struck me like a slap in the face. That was right. If this was the Pole, then we were the first people here— Matt first and me second. I was the second person to reach the North Pole. Oatah was third. Seegloo fourth. Commander Peary was fifth. If this was the Pole, his dream of reaching it was complete. His dream of reaching it *first,* however, was gone forever.

I almost hoped we hadn't reached it, that the Pole was another half mile or mile away and he could lead. It was his dream, his lifelong work. He had been separated from his family for years at a time, lost eight toes, and almost his life. It just didn't seem fair that it wasn't him.

"Gather around!" Commander Peary ordered.

I looked at Matt. "I guess we're going to find out."

Oatah and Seegloo were tending to the dogs. Slowly they came over and the four of us stood in front of the Commander.

"I have just taken readings," he began, telling us what we all already knew. "And according to my calculations, we are now standing at latitude ninety degrees north. In every way you look the direction is south. We stand upon the nail, upon the very top of the world . . . on the Pole!"

I didn't know whether I was supposed to cheer or offer my congratulations or my apologies for robbing him—

accidentally—of being the first. I just stood there in silence.

"The Pole at last! The prize of three centuries. My dream and goal for twenty-three years. Mine at last. *I am the first man to reach the Pole!*"

The first? I looked over at Matt. He was looking at the Commander.

"I cannot bring myself to realize it. It all seems so simple and commonplace, but it is mine! Matthew, bring me the marker!"

Matt went over to Commander Peary's sledge. He pulled the canvas back farther and brought out a flag attached to a metal pole. It was the Stars and Stripes— the flag of the United States of America.

Matt brought back the pole and a mallet. He held the pole up, then drove it into the ice. He hit it again and again until the pole was solidly in the ice. He stepped back then and the wind caught the flag and it shot straight back to reveal the red, white, and blue. Commander Peary came to attention and saluted the flag.

"We will only be here for a short time, perhaps an hour, before we start back. In that time I will mark readings and record my thoughts and feelings in my journal. I suggest you all drink in the moment of our success. Without you, my triumph would not have been possible," Commander Peary said.

He walked away from the flag all the way to his sledge. His walk was awkward but there was a pride in the straightness of his back. It was like all of the weariness had been washed away in those brief minutes. He sat down on the edge of the sledge and pulled out his journal and began to write.

I looked up at Matt. He was still standing beside the flag, staring at it. He looked over at me and smiled.

"We did it," I said.

He nodded. "Yes, we did. Because of what we have done, Commander Peary has become the first man to reach the Pole."

"But he wasn't," I said. "*You* were, and I was second and then there was Oatah and Seegloo—"

"Keep your voice down," he hissed.

I knew the Commander was far enough away that he couldn't have heard me, but still I lowered my voice. "He *wasn't* the first," I repeated softly.

"He planned the expedition, secured the funds, was the Commander. The only reason we are here now is because of him."

"Maybe the only reason he's here is 'cause of us, 'cause of you. Besides, no matter who did the plannin', four people arrived before him."

Matt shook his head. "You're just a boy, and Oatah and Seegloo are Eskimos."

"But *you* were the first man."

"The first man was Peary. I'm just his servant, his Negro servant. I don't count."

"Of course ya count and counted first and—"

"Stop!" he said, softly but firmly, cutting off my sentence. "Let's not repeat that. Not now and not ever. No matter what you say, or what I know, I also know who will be credited in the history books. It won't be me or any of the Eskimos. It will be Commander Peary.

Why do you think he didn't want Captain Bartlett along?" Matt asked.

"Because he wanted him to mark the trail back."

"Many could have marked that trail. The reason was that if Captain Bartlett had come along he could have laid claim to being the first man at the Pole. But you and I and the Eskimos can make no such claim."

"But . . . but . . . that doesn't seem fair."

"Life is not necessarily fair."

Those were the same words used by Captain Bartlett.

"Do you think the history books will record my name instead of Commander Peary's?"

"Well . . . I don't know."

"I do. Peary discovered the North Pole. He is the only man who has set foot here. We are merely his servants. Now, if you'll excuse me, I have to prepare for our return."

He walked away, leaving Oatah and Seegloo and me standing beside the flag.

"There is nothing here," Oatah said, and Seegloo nodded in agreement.

"What do you mean?" I asked.

"Nothing here but ice. Why did we come here if there is nothing but ice?"

"I guess because nobody had ever done it before. To prove that we *could* do it."

Oatah shook his head. "I don't understand. Why work so hard to get to no place nobody ever was or ever should be? No sense."

Seegloo said something in Inuktitut and Oatah nodded his head enthusiastically in agreement.

"What did he say?" I asked.

"He said he expected more, something different. Nothing different here. Nothing more. Just ice. It's time to go home."

Oatah and Seegloo walked off, leaving me alone. I put one hand on the metal pole as the flag fluttered noisily in the stiff breeze. Around me in all directions was south. And in all those directions there was nothing but ice and snow and cold. We were standing on the top of the world, a place no one had ever stood before. I took a deep breath and inhaled the cool, clean air that had never been inhaled by another human.

Peary was right. We *had* made history. And I knew that Matt was right, too. Those history books wouldn't mention his name or mine as being the first person. They would say "Commander Robert Peary, conqueror of the North Pole." And somewhere in small print, if at all, there would be a note saying that he was accompanied by two Eskimos and his faithful Negro servant, Matthew, and a boy from the *Roosevelt*. Maybe it would mention my name, or maybe just say "a boy." Then again, it really didn't matter what the history books said. I knew the truth, and so did Matt. It didn't matter what the books would say because I knew what they *should* say: "Matthew Hensen—hero, master sledge driver, friend to the Eskimos, man of honour and loyalty and integrity, and the first man to reach the North Pole."

And I was second.

Author's Note

The writing of historical fiction is always a curious dance between those parts that are fiction and those that are history. Captain Robert Bartlett, Commander Robert Peary, and Matthew Hensen were all real men, and this novel is based on their attempt, under Peary's command, to reach the North Pole in 1909.

Despite the passing of close to one hundred years, controversy still remains. Did Robert Peary and his small, final assault party, including Matthew Hensen and three Inuit, reach the Pole? While there is a great deal of evidence that both supports and refutes this claim, I am certain of some things. These were incredibly brave men who possessed determination and endurance that was almost beyond human limits.

What also appears clear is that, since Matthew Hensen broke trail for Peary through the final marches to the Pole, he reached the Pole first. Hensen's place in history, as with the Inuit who also accompanied Peary, was downgraded because they were not, in 1909, seen as being men fully because they were not white.

While all are heroes, and Peary was certainly the commander, mastermind, and driving force behind the expedition to the Pole, if they did in fact reach their goal, then I believe the honour of first man at 90 North belongs to Matthew Hensen.